Ski Trip
Trouble

THE date him or dump him? SERIES

The Campfire Crush

The Dance Dilemma

Ski Trip Trouble

date him or dump him?

Ski Trip Trouble

A Choose Your Boyfriend Book

Cylin Busby

BLOOMSBURY
CHILDREN'S
BOOKS

Published by Bloomsbury U.S.A. Children's Books
175 Fifth Avenue, New York, NY 10010
Distributed to the trade by Holtzbrinck Publishers

Library of Congress Cataloging-in-Publication Data
Busby, Cylin.
Ski trip trouble / by Cylin Busby.—1st U.S. ed.
p.   cm.   —(Date him or dump him? A choose your boyfriend book ; 3)
Summary: As a teenaged girl on a school ski trip who is attracted to more than one
admiring boy, the reader makes choices to determine the outcome of the story.
ISBN-13: 978-1-59990-106-0 • ISBN-10: 1-59990-106-4
1. Plot-your-own stories. [1. Dating (Social customs)—Fiction.
2. Skis and skiing—Fiction. 3. Plot-your-own stories.] I. Title.
PZ7.B9556Sk 2007   [Fic]—dc22   2007002594

First U.S. Edition 2007
Book designed and typeset by Amelia May Anderson
Printed in the U.S.A. by Quebecor World Fairfield
2 4 6 8 10 9 7 5 3 1

BLOOMSBURY
CHILDREN'S
BOOKS

For the Jennies at the JCC
(and Molli, too)

Ski Trip Trouble

It's another cold, gray day when you get to school on Thursday morning. Winter break is just two weeks away, but before you can relax and take some time off from school, there are all those end-of-the-semester tests, papers, and projects due. Thank goodness it's the school ski trip this weekend, otherwise you'd be going out of your mind with stress! Before you even go to your first class, you head over to the main bulletin board to check out the sign-up sheet for the ski trip one more time.

"I can't believe it's finally here!" your friend Heather says as she comes up behind you. "Tomorrow—no school, we just hit the mountain. I cannot wait!"

"Look at this," you say, pointing to one name on the list.

"Dan's going? Wasn't he, like, in love with you last year?" Heather jokes, and you have to laugh.

"I guess so." You grin. "But now I hear he likes somebody else."

Heather blushes. "I don't know about that!"

"Oh please, he follows you around everywhere, just like he used to do with me," you say, but Heather just looks down at her shoes shyly. "And I'm getting the feeling that you might like him back...."

"Maybe just a little," she admits, pinching her thumb and forefinger together.

"I guess a romantic ski trip to the snowy slopes will help you figure it out!" you joke, hooking your arm through hers. "We better get to class," you say, just as the warning bell rings.

"Did you hear that Marshall High is also going to Mount Frost this weekend?" Heather asks you with a sly grin.

"You know I did," you say back, "because you're the one who told me!"

"I just can't help wondering if a certain former crush is going to be there," Heather goes on.

"Look, I haven't seen Mitch since he moved away over the summer," you explain. "It's been months." You stop outside the door to your class-room. "And just because his new school is going on this trip, it doesn't mean *he's* going to be there."

"Uh-huh," Heather says, cocking her head to one side. "So the thought hasn't even crossed your mind? You and Mitch, sipping hot chocolate, talking about those long days at the pool last summer, that time when you almost kissed..."

You move to swat her with your backpack, but she jumps back just in time. "Knock it off!" You laugh. "Seriously, what if he's not even there?"

"I have a feeling he will be," Heather teases as the final bell rings. "Eek! I'm late!"

"Call me tonight—let's talk about what we're going to pack, okay?" you yell after her as she races down the hall.

"Okay! Later," she yells back.

Very early the next morning—when it's still practi-cally dark out—you meet up with Heather and all the other students going on the ski trip.

"I feel like a snowman in this thing," Heather says, patting the front of her big, puffy white jacket.

"I know what you mean," you say, zipping up

your own coat. Mrs. Bulow, the teacher who organized the trip, comes over to the group crowded around the bus.

"Everyone, listen up!" she says, clapping her gloved hands together. "I'm going to be the head chaperone on this trip. If you have any problems or issues, come to me."

"I have an issue," Heather whispers to you. "I'm freezing to death! When do we get on the bus?"

You can feel your feet getting numb—it *is* a really cold morning.

"We have two other teachers coming along on the trip, and we have four seniors from the school who have volunteered to be junior chaperones." Mrs. Bulow points to the guys standing next to her. "This is James," she says, introducing a tall guy with dark hair. "And this is Glenn," she goes on, "and Max," she says, pointing to a blond guy in a puffy down vest standing next to her. "And, of course, Cathy." She motions to the petite girl on her other side. "All of these students are seniors and have been on the school ski trip in the past. And they are all excellent skiers."

"Excellent indeed…," you hear Heather murmur next to you.

"Shhhhh," you whisper back, but she's right—the guys are all amazingly hot.

"What?" Heather says. "Like you wouldn't die for that guy to ride the chairlift with you?" She nods at the dark-haired senior.

You take another glance at him—just when he happens to look your way! You quickly look down.

"Busted!" Heather says under her breath. You feel your cheeks turning even redder as Mrs. Bulow goes on.

"Respect the junior chaperones. They are not just fellow students; they are here to look out for you. Treat them exactly the same way you would treat us teachers," she says, motioning to the two other teachers standing near her.

Heather starts doing a little dance from one foot to the other, trying to keep warm, just as Mrs. Bulow happens to look over. "Does anyone need to use the bathroom before we go?" she asks, and a few of the boys in the group start laughing. "It is a two-hour trip," she says, looking pointedly at you and Heather.

Heather stops hopping. "Oh man, could she embarrass us more?"

"I know it's cold out here—let's line up and

climb on the bus!" Mrs. Bulow finally says, and everyone races for the door. When you and Heather finally make your way up the stairs into the bus, almost every seat is taken. "Here?" Heather says, pointing to a seat right behind the driver. It's not exactly the best seat, but you don't really have any other choice—the bus is totally packed.

When everyone is sitting, Mrs. Bulow comes onboard. "We have a tiny problem," she starts. "I need to ride on the bus, too, but as you can see, it's full. So I need someone to give me their seat and ride up to the mountain in the van with the junior chaperones."

"Let's do it," Heather whispers to you, nudging your arm.

"We'll volunteer," you say quickly. "Heather and I don't mind."

"Yeah, no problem," Heather agrees, standing up and grabbing her backpack.

"Sorry, girls, I only need *one* of you to give up your seat," Mrs. Bulow points out. "And there's only room for one person in the van, too. But if you don't mind going alone"—she looks directly at you—"this seat *would* be perfect for me, right up front where I can keep an eye on everyone."

You look over at Heather. "It's up to you," she says, though you're sure she'd rather not have to sit by Mrs. Bulow for the two-hour bus ride. You can't help thinking about that junior chaperone, James, and how cool it would be to get to know him better. You look back at Heather. It *is* just a ride up the mountain, after all, and you'll get to hang out with Heather for the rest of the weekend....

"Let's get a move on here!" the bus driver says, turning around to look at you. "In or out, missy?" He pulls the handle to open the bus door, and a rush of cold air comes in, hitting your face. You take a deep breath and decide to...

Stay on the bus with Heather. Go to 8.

Join the junior chaperones in the van. Go to 10.

"I think I'd rather stay on the bus with my friend," you tell Mrs. Bulow.

"I'll go," a guy sitting across from you quickly volunteers.

"Perfect!" Mrs. Bulow says.

"See you up there, suckers!" the guy yells as he goes out the door of the bus.

"What a loser," Heather whispers to you.

"He's probably right, though—the van will make it up there a lot faster than this old bus," you say.

"Are you wishing you'd gone in the van?" Heather asks, looking hurt.

"No, I'm just saying...," you start, but then notice someone leaning over you—it's Dan.

"Hey," he says, pushing his shaggy blond hair back from his eyes. "I was just wondering if maybe I could sit with Heather," he asks, looking at you.

"Um..." You're about to say no, but then notice that Heather is giving you a hopeful look. Maybe

8

you should have gone in the van after all! "Sure, I can move," you mumble.

"Great!" Heather says.

"I was sitting right back there." Dan points back to the only empty seat, and you make your way down the aisle as he sits next to Heather. When you get to the back of the bus, you realize that Dan had been sitting with this cute guy—all you know about him is that he skipped a grade and he's supposed to be super smart.

"Is it okay if I sit here?" you ask him. "Dan wanted to move up front."

9

Go to 16.

"Okay, I'll ride in the van," you tell Mrs. Bulow. You hear Heather let out a sigh, so you turn to her. "I'll see you up there," you explain. "Please don't be mad."

"I'm not." Heather smiles. "Just wish I was coming, too. Say hi to James for me, 'kay?" She winks.

"No problem," you say as you go down the stairs and leave the bus. The driver follows you and opens the luggage compartment. You see your bag right on top and grab it. "Thanks," you tell the driver with a wave as he climbs back onto the bus.

You walk over to the van and hear music blasting out of the open doors. "Hi! Mrs. Bulow asked me to ride up with you guys," you tell the girl junior chaperone.

"Cool," she says, grabbing your bag and tossing it into the back of the van. "I'm Cathy. You can sit with me while this maniac drives." She gives James a little punch in the arm.

"Maniac on the slopes," James corrects her.

"Behind the wheel, never." He grins over at you. "Hey, I'm James," he says, putting out his hand, and you tell him your name.

"Let's go, people!" says Mr. Abbott, one of the teachers chaperoning the trip, motioning everyone into the van. You sit next to Cathy in the first row of backseats, while the two other seniors sit behind you. When James goes to sit in the driver's seat, Mr. Abbot says, "Not so fast," and grabs the keys from him. "I'll be doing the driving."

James grumbles but sits in the passenger seat and instantly starts messing with the CD player. "Okay, passengers, what do we want to hear? Some death rock, acid beats?"

You let out a laugh because you assume he's joking—he doesn't really listen to that type of music, does he? In a second, you realize you're wrong as James slips in a disc of the worst music you've ever heard.

"These guys and their heavy metal," Cathy grumbles to you over the loud music. She puts on her own headphones and starts listening to her MP3 player, looking out the window. By the time Mr. Abbott pulls the van out onto the freeway, you already have a headache.

"This album is so rad—this is the best ski music ever!" you hear Glenn, the other junior chaperone, say from behind you.

"Get ready to party!" James says loudly, and Mr. Abbott shoots him a look.

"Can you please turn that noise down?" Mr. Abbott asks. "I'm trying to drive, here."

"Noise?" James says. "This is one of the greatest heavy metal albums of all time!" He turns around in his seat and looks at you. "You dig it, right? I mean, how awesome are these guitar licks?" James plays air guitar along with the song for a second, and you almost burst out laughing. Even if his taste in music is terrible, he's still adorable.

12

"It's not exactly my type of music," you tell him, smiling.

"When we get up to the mountain, we'll teach you how to really party," James says knowingly. "Right, dude?" he says to Glenn, and gives him a thumbs-up.

"Righteous!" Glenn yells over the music.

Are these guys for real?

"Oh no," you hear Mr. Abbott say suddenly as the van starts making a funny thumping sound— *chug-chug-chug*—and then it stops altogether!

"Sorry, guys, I thought this van might give us trouble," Mr. Abbott says as he pulls over to the side of the highway. The van comes to a stop, and Mr. Abbott turns around. "I'll go have a look at the engine, but I think we may need to call a tow truck." His face looks glum as he climbs out of the van. He lifts the hood, and black smoke comes billowing out of the engine!

"That's not good," James jokes.

Mr. Abbott pokes his head back into the van for a second. "The bus is coming up the hill right behind us, so if any of you want to flag down the driver and get on, feel free. This looks like it's going to take a while," he explains.

You want to get up to the mountain so that you can ski this afternoon with your friends, but you were also looking forward to this road trip with James the cutie. You look over to him for a second. "I'm staying, man. The bus is for losers!" he says.

"Here comes the bus. Anyone want me to flag it down?" Mr. Abbott says again, and you decide to…

Stay and wait for the repairs on the van. Go to 18.

Flag down the bus and squeeze on. Go to 21.

"Great," the guy says. You tap Zac on the shoulder, and when he slips off his headphones, you quickly explain what's up.

"So I'll see you later," you say as you move over to sit by Molly.

"Definitely." Zac grins back. Looks like you've made at least one new friend on this trip already!

Once you get settled into your new seat, you turn to Molly. "You're new at school, right?" After the words are out of your mouth, you feel silly. Obviously she's new!

"Yeah," she says, nodding. "We used to live a couple of towns over, so it's not that different."

"But it must have been hard to leave all your friends," you continue.

"That wasn't easy, but I still see them sometimes. Actually, some of my old friends from middle school go to Marshall now. One of my best friends, Sierra, is going on this trip—I'm psyched to meet her up there."

"How cool," you say, but just the mention of the

other high school instantly makes you think of Mitch. "I have a friend from last year who goes to Marshall. So maybe he'll be there, too," you tell her.

She raises her eyebrows. "Friend? Or boy-friend?" she says with a grin.

"Well..." You feel your cheeks flush as you struggle to answer.

"You don't have to explain," Molly says, pulling her long blond hair into a high ponytail. "I know all about those kinds of friends!"

You realize that Molly is actually really easy to talk to—she's funny and super nice, too. "When we get up there, do you want to room together?" she asks. "I don't really have any friends on this trip, so I was just going to stay with whoever was left."

You had been planning to stay with Heather and her friend Carrie, but it might be fun to room with a new friend—especially one who has Marshall connections! And Heather is so wrapped up with her crush on Dan, she probably wouldn't even notice...but then again, she is your best friend....

15

You'd rather stay with Heather. Go to 187.

You want to room with the new girl, Molly. Go to 29.

"Sure," he says, "I don't think we've ever met, but I'm Zac." You tell him your name and he quickly responds, "Oh, I know who you are—I thought that project you did in English last week was really amazing."

"Thanks." You smile. You had thought it was pretty cool, but none of your friends even mentioned it to you. "So, you skipped a grade or something, right?" you ask him.

"Yeah, the teachers thought it might be a good idea, so I was bumped up," he says, looking out the window. It seems like he doesn't really want to talk about it, but you're so curious.

"How is it going? Is it really hard to keep up?" you ask.

"I'm only a year younger than everybody else, so it's not that big a deal," he explains. "But *some* people want to make it a big deal, you know?"

You nod and glance over at the popular kids, all sitting together in a group. "Yeah, I know what you mean," you tell him.

"Anyway," he says, looking at your MP3 player, "what are you listening to?"

You two start talking about—and listening to—music, and before you know it, a half hour has gone by. You're listening to his MP3 player, and he's checking out yours, when the guy sitting across the aisle from you leans over and taps your shoulder.

"Hey, would you mind switching seats with me?" he asks. "Zac is my tutor at school and I need to ask him some homework questions."

You glance over at Zac, but he's got headphones on and hasn't noticed anything. You look back at the guy and see that he's sitting with Molly, the new girl at school. You've noticed her in your art class, and she seems really cool. This could be your chance to meet her. But you also really like sitting with Zac and getting to know him.

You tell the guy:

"Sure, I'll switch seats with you." Go to 14.

"Sorry, Zac's busy right now. You'll have to ask him later."
    Go to 189.

17

"That's okay, Mr. Abbott," you say. "I'll just wait with everyone else." As the bus roars by, a few kids make faces through the windows. So what if they'll get up the mountain before you? At least you get to hang with a group of cool seniors!

Before too long, the repair crew shows up with a tow truck. "Sorry, mister," the driver says to Mr. Abbott. "This van isn't going anywhere. We can have a rental vehicle sent out, but we'll have to tow this one back to the garage."

"Okay," Mr. Abbott says. "I guess we don't really have much choice. Everyone please get your bags out of the back."

Cathy opens the back of the van and starts piling up the bags on the side of the road, but as she puts one big duffel bag down, you hear a loud *clink* and the sound of glass breaking. "Oops," Cathy says, cringing, as a dark syrupy liquid starts leaking through the bag. "What's that?"

In a few seconds, there's a puddle of something

under the bag, and it smells sweet—and strange, like…

"Is that what I think it is?" Mr. Abbott says, taking a sniff. He unzips the bag to reveal a four-pack of wine coolers, two of the bottles broken. "Whose bag is this?" he asks, and no one says anything. "Yours?" He turns to Glenn.

Glenn just looks down.

"Glenn, show me which bag is yours," Mr. Abbott says, and he sounds angry.

"Hmm," Glenn says, looking over the bags. "I really can't remember right now."

Mr. Abbott glares at him. "Cathy, which one is yours?" he asks.

"Gosh, Mr. Abbott," she says, "I can't tell; they all look alike." She gives James a nudge. You know what they're doing—no one is going to take the blame.

Mr. Abbott points to you. "Which bag is yours? And stop playing games!"

You look down at the bags, then up at James, who gives you a sly smile. If you play along, then maybe no one will get in trouble. But you shouldn't get in trouble, anyway—you didn't do anything wrong! Do you want to cover for James and his friends, or tell the truth and point out your bag?

You lie and say you can't remember which bag is yours. Go to 23.

You show Mr. Abbott your bag. Go to 25.

"I want to get on the bus," you tell Mr. Abbott, and he quickly puts his hand out to wave down the driver.

"Aw, man, are you for real?" James says, obviously disappointed in you. "I thought you were cool."

You're about to say something to him when the bus pulls over and the driver opens the door, so you just turn and say a quick "'bye" as you climb aboard.

"Yeah, whatever," James says, looking away.

When you get on the bus, the first thing you notice is that Mrs. Bulow isn't sitting with Heather anymore—instead, Dan is!

"Hey," you say to them.

"What happened?" Heather looks really surprised to see you. "Your ride didn't work out?" "Something like that," you say, rolling your eyes. "It's a long story!"

"Well, I would have saved your seat, but..." She glances over at Dan, then back to you.

"Don't worry about it," you say, shooting her a

grin as you move past them to the back of the bus. You see Mrs. Bulow sitting back there.

"We have one open seat back here, actually," Mrs. Bulow says. "One student felt a little sick before we left the parking lot," she whispers, "so he stayed behind." You can see the only open seat is next to a cute guy you don't really know. He's supposed to be super smart and skipped a grade last year.

"Um, okay if I sit here?" you ask him.

22

Go to 16.

ou look up at Mr. Abbott and play along. "I can't really tell which one is mine," you say, and glance over at James. He grins back at you just as Mr. Abbott turns to him.

"Oh, you think this is funny?" Mr. Abbott questions. James just looks down and pulls his hat lower on his head. "I saw that smirk! This isn't a joke," Mr. Abbott says, looking at each of you in turn. "Underage drinking is serious. You *know* that you are not allowed to have alcohol on this trip!" he yells.

Mr. Abbott kicks the brown duffel bag with the bottles in it. "I want to know whose bag this is RIGHT NOW," he orders.

You look down at your snow boots, feeling terrible. You've never gotten in trouble for something this serious before.

"Okay, nobody wants to talk?" Mr. Abbott says after a few minutes of silence. "Great. Then nobody here will go on the trip. When the rental van comes, I'll drive you back to school and you can call your parents. I'm sure they'll be very proud of you."

You look over at James. Why doesn't he just say the bag was his? It's not fair for all of you to be kicked off the trip because of him! "Here comes the van now," Mr. Abbott says, pointing down the road. "Last chance…"

Cathy and Glenn just look down, and you glance around at the group of seniors. How could you have thought these people were cool, just because they're older? You're suddenly wishing that you'd just stayed on the bus!

"Okay, that's it," Mr. Abbott says, shaking his head. "Everyone in the van. We'll sort this out when we get back to the school."

Looks like your ski trip has ended—before it even had a chance to start!

END

If you want to rethink your decision, go back to 18.

24

"My bag is...," you force out, "the purple one." You look over at James and can tell that he's not happy with you.

"Okay, so I know you're still going on the trip," Mr. Abbott says. "Does anyone else want to tell me which bag is theirs?"

"That one's mine," Cathy speaks up, pointing to a black duffel. She looks over at James for a second, then looks down.

"That's two. Anyone else?" Mr. Abbott looks around the group. "Here comes the rental van now—last chance..." He looks right at James.

One of the other senior guys, Max, points to a green backpack. "That's mine," he says quietly.

"Fine, then, we'll all head back to the school and drop off anyone who 'can't remember' which bag is theirs, then you three will travel up to the mountain with me," Mr. Abbott explains. "I'll let the principal sort this out," he says, picking up the drippy brown duffel bag.

After Mr. Abbott drives Glenn and James back

to school, you're on your way again, back on the freeway, only this time the trip feels very different. There's no music; the van is silent. Cathy just looks out the window, and so you put on your MP3 player. You feel terrible about what happened, even though it's not your fault. How could you have been so wrong about James? He turned out to be a real loser.

You fall asleep, and the next thing you know, you're at Mount Frost! Suddenly, the whole world is covered in snow, even the tall pine trees surrounding the resort. When Mr. Abbott pulls up behind the three-story lodge, you can see that most of the kids from school are already hanging out on the huge wraparound deck, putting on their ski gear or just having a hot chocolate. You're bummed that you've already missed the first few hours of the ski trip—and you hope that you can still room with Heather.

You climb out of the van and feel your boots crunch on the fresh snow. You take in a deep breath of the cold mountain air just as you hear someone say, "Hey, Mr. Abbott!"

"Hi, Zac, how was the bus ride up?" Mr. Abbott

asks a young-looking guy with light brown hair.

"Loud!" the guy laughs, and glances over at you. "We were wondering where you guys were—what happened?"

"It's a long story," Mr. Abbott starts. "Why don't we get these folks inside," he says, turning to open the back of the van.

Zac grabs your bag right away. "I've got it," he says. "Let me help you. I'm already unpacked."

You smile at him—what a sweet guy! When he smiles back, you notice he's got a mouthful of braces, which makes him look even younger. How old is he? You don't really know him at all, but you've heard he's super smart and that he skipped a grade last year.

You follow Zac and Mr. Abbott into the lodge and up to the main desk. "I think everyone who came in on the bus already has a room," Zac tells you, handing your bag to you. "Except my friend Molly was still looking for a roommate if you want to board with her," he explains, pointing over to a blond girl you recognize from school.

"She's new, right?" you ask, and Zac nods.

"She's really cool; she just doesn't know anyone

yet. Or you can look around for your friends, but like I said, I think everyone else on the bus was assigned rooms."

It sounds like Heather probably already picked a room with someone else, so you could room with the new girl. It might actually be fun to change it up—besides, Heather's going to be so obsessed with Dan on this trip, you're not sure you even want to room with her. But maybe you should look around for Heather and ask her, just to be sure...she is your best friend, after all.

You'll take a chance and room with the new girl, Molly. Go to 180.

You'd rather room with Heather. Go to 182.

"It must be down here," Molly says, leading the way to your room. "My friend, Sierra, the one that I told you about, is already checked in. I heard their bus got here early."

You round the corner and run into a really tall girl with short dark hair. "Sierra!" Molly screams, and hugs her hard. "Hey, this is Sierra!" she says, and introduces you.

"Come on, our room is down this way—and it's great!" Sierra says.

As you follow her down the hall, you decide to ask her about your old crush. "So, you go to Marshall.... Do you know this guy named Mitch? He would have been new at your school this year."

Sierra turns to look at you. "No, I don't think so," she says. "Here's our room." She stops outside a door and reaches into her pocket. "Now where did I put that..." She reaches into her other pocket. "Oh no, I think I left the key inside!"

"That's okay, we can just go down to the desk and get another one," Molly says. "I'll go, you guys stay here and get to know each other—be right back!" She dashes off for the stairs.

"I'm sorry, I'm always doing stuff like that," Sierra says, looking embarrassed.

"No big deal," you say, and drop your duffel bag on the floor. You sit with your back to the wall, and Sierra plops down next to you.

Two guys walk by in the hallway, and one of them almost trips over your feet. You look up and suddenly see Mitch!

"How weird, I was just talking about you, Mitch!" You jump up and give him a hug. He looks exactly the same—with his shaggy brown hair and ocean-blue eyes.

"Hey, you," Mitch says, hugging you back. "And hi, Sierra. You two know each other?" he asks.

"We just met," Sierra says. So she does know Mitch after all. Why didn't she say so in the first place?

"This your room?" Mitch asks, looking at the door number.

"Yeah, we're just sort of…," you start to say.

"Locked out," Sierra finishes for you. "Totally my fault."

Mitch laughs and shakes his head. "Already?

The weekend has just begun, ladies!"

"Hey, dude," a tall guy comes up behind Mitch and says, "you ready to roll?"

"Yeah, absolutely." Mitch turns to go. "If you can't get into your room, come swing by ours. I'm in three-twelve." He grins at you.

"Um, okay," you say, blushing. "Maybe later."

After Mitch walks away with his friends, you look over to Sierra. "I guess I do know him," she explains. "But at our school, he goes by Tom." She looks confused.

"Oh right—his name is Tom Mitchell, but everyone at our school just called him Mitch. It's his nickname or whatever." You smile. "How funny!"

"Well, you might not like to hear this," Sierra says, whispering, "but he's dating a friend of mine—and they're super serious. Did you guys used to go out or something?"

You feel your heart practically stop beating. "What?" you say. "Are you sure?" Just then you see Molly heading down the hall toward you, waving the key over her head.

"As far as I know, they're still going out," Sierra says, standing up. "Are you bummed?" she asks you, but you can't even answer her. You're crushed—Mitch has a girlfriend? Then why did he give you a hug and ask you to come by his room? Maybe Sierra is wrong. You should probably go and talk to him for yourself and find out what's up.

"Here we go," Molly says, opening the door. You walk into the room behind Sierra and Molly and drop your bag on the floor. "Should we hit the slopes right away?" she asks, looking at you and Sierra.

You let out a sigh—you're feeling so down. What should you do first? Go and see Mitch and find out what's really up with him, or just wait to run into him later?

You decide to stop by Mitch's room. Go to 40.

You'll just wait and maybe see him later. Go to 42.

"So this is it," Heather says, opening the door to the room. It's small and dark, and you see only *two* beds.

"Wait, I thought you said that Carrie was going to stay with us, too," you say to her.

"She is," Heather says. "There's a third bed here; it's called a Murphy bed." She walks over to the wall and shows you a place where there's a metal handle attached to what looks like a big closet door. "See, you just have to pull this...." She grunts as she pulls down hard on the handle, but nothing happens. "Well, it's supposed to work."

"Hey, girlies!" you hear Carrie say as she comes in the room and drops her duffel bag on the floor. "I love it." She throws herself across one bed and stretches out. "Wait..." She sits up and looks around. "Where's the third bed?"

"We're trying to figure it out," you tell her, pointing to the handle on the wall.

"Oh cool," Carrie says, "a Murphy bed! I love it. Let's put it down."

You and Heather step back and let Carrie try. "Ugh!" she groans. "This thing won't budge. It's supposed to swing open and be a bed," she explains.

"We already know that." Heather sounds exasperated. "It just won't move! Here, let me help," she says, putting her hands next to Carrie's. You grab Heather around the waist and pull back, giving her some extra leverage.

"Okay, on the count of three," you say, and you all pull—until Heather's hand slips, and she falls backward, right on top of you!

"Ouch!" you squeal, but you're not hurt. Carrie plops down on the ground, too.

"There must be a button or a lock or something," Heather says.

"I don't see anything," you say. "Should I go and get Mrs. Bulow to help us?"

"I have a better idea." Heather grins. "Why not Mitch? He's big and strong!"

"Heather!" you say, but you have to laugh. It's definitely not the worst idea...but what if you go to ask him for help and find that you can't talk again—you'd just make a fool out of yourself for the second time today! At the same time, it is a good excuse to connect with him, and show him your room....

You want to ask Mitch for help. Go to 44.
You'd rather ask Mrs. Bulow for help. Go to 46.

ou move back up front and sit with Heather, and after a few minutes, you wish you'd stayed with Zac. All Heather wants to talk about is Dan!

After about half an hour of the Dan marathon, you really can't take it anymore. "Can we talk about something other than Dan?" you ask her, finally.

"Fine," Heather says, acting huffy. "Let's talk about your little nerd boy, what's his name?"

"Who, Zac?" you ask.

"Yeah, how old is he? And those braces!" she says, laughing.

"He's only one year younger than us," you point out. "And he's actually a really nice guy."

"Right," Heather says, and shoots you a funny look. "You *are* joking?"

"No, I'm serious," you start to explain, just as the bus turns a corner and drives into the ski resort. Everyone cheers as you enter the winter wonderland. Snow is everywhere—on the ground, on the trees, even on the roof of the lodge. You can see tons of kids already out on the slopes.

"Oh, I forgot to tell you," Heather says quickly, "I told Carrie that she could room with us."

"Heather!" you say, shooting her a look. "You know I don't get along with her."

"If I can put up with you hanging out with nerdy what's-his-name back there, you can put up with my friend," Heather reasons.

You're so annoyed, but what can you do? Then you remember that Zac had mentioned that his friend Molly—who is new at the school—didn't have anyone to room with. When he told you, you assumed that you'd be rooming with Heather, but now you're not so sure you want to. Should you take a chance on the new girl, or just stay with Heather and Carrie?

You choose to room with the new girl. Go to 184.

You decide to stay with Heather and Carrie. Go to 187.

"That's okay, guys," you tell Dan and Heather. "I don't mind sitting here. I'll see you when we get to the mountain."

"Okay, suit yourself," Heather says, walking back to her seat with Dan trailing behind her.

As all the other kids get back on the bus, you see Zac coming down the aisle. He gives you a big metal grin, and you have to smile back. Sure, he's younger than you and your friends, but really nice and actually not bad-looking, either. You scoot over so that he can sit down.

You two talk for the rest of the trip, mostly about the bands that you both like and movies that you've seen recently. Before you know it, the bus turns down a snow-covered road toward the resort. You can see the peak of the mountain, with lots of skiers already making their way down the slopes, and it looks amazing!

"Hey, I meant to ask you something," Zac says. "My friend Molly doesn't have anyone to room with—she's new—do you think you might want to stay with her? She's really cool, I promise!" he says.

"I told Heather I'd stay with her," you say quickly. "But…" You think for second. Maybe it would fun to stay with someone else—and you like Zac so much, you're sure his friend would be really cool, too. You look up to the front of the bus and see Dan and Heather sitting close together. Would she really care if you stayed with someone else?

You decide to meet Zac's friend Molly. Go to 180.

You'd rather just stay with your friend Heather. Go to 187.

"I'm going to swing by Mitch's room, really fast, just to catch up," you tell Sierra and Molly.

Sierra looks up from where she's unpacking. "Why? I told you he has a girlfriend."

"I just want to say hi—," you start to explain, but Molly cuts you off.

"Are you going to come back and ski with us? Once we get unpacked, we're hitting the slopes," she says.

"Yeah, I'll be right back," you promise as you shoot out the door and down the hall to Mitch's room. You knock on the door, and his roommate, the tall guy with buzz-cut dark hair, answers.

"Hi—you must be looking for Tom," he says.

"Tom?" you ask, then remember that's what people call him at his new school. "Um, right."

"Yeah, you're the girl from the hallway," the guy says. "I'm Travis. Come on in." When you walk into the room, the first thing you notice is piles of skiing and snowboarding equipment all over the place. These guys are definitely not neat freaks!

"Hey!" Mitch says, obviously happy to see you. "I hope you're not still locked out," he jokes. You look into his dark blue eyes for a second and feel funny, like you can't breathe—the same way you used to feel last year every time you two hung out.

"Naw, we finally got into our room," you say, looking away fast.

"Cool, so go grab your stuff and come ski with me and Travis," Mitch says, picking up his hat and gloves. "We'll meet you at the chairlift in ten?" he asks.

"Um…" You think for a second. You came to find out if Mitch really has a girlfriend, but you don't feel comfortable asking him with Travis standing there. Plus, you did tell the girls that you'd ski with them. But maybe if you ski with Mitch, you can find a way to talk later? Finally, you say:

41

"I can't, I told the girls I'd ski with them—sorry." Go to 42.

"Sure, I'd love to! See you at the chairlift!" Go to 48.

When you're getting changed into your ski clothes with Molly and Sierra, you can't believe the amazing outfits they brought to ski in.

"Wow, you guys are serious," you say, looking them over when they're suited up.

"You like it?" Molly says, spinning around in her fitted red-and-black snowsuit. "I think Sierra's is way cooler," she admits, pointing to Sierra's fitted white suit with a big black belt.

"Come on, get ready and join us!" Sierra says, pulling a puffy white hat down over her dark, pixie-cut hair. She looks adorable!

"I don't know, you guys, I was just going to rent a snowsuit. I don't think you're going to want to be seen with me!" you laugh.

"Why rent? I have an extra jacket that would fit you," Sierra says, digging through her huge duffel bag. In a minute, she pulls out a funky silver jacket and tosses it to you. "Try it on!"

You slip into the jacket and look in the mirror. It's short and fitted, coming only to your waist, with a high collar that hugs your neck as you zip it up.

"Hot!" Molly says. "You *have to* wear it!"

You do look pretty good—who wouldn't in this thing? It probably cost a fortune! "This is too nice to wear skiing...," you start to say to Sierra.

"Please," she says, "I have, like, five more at home."

And Molly nods to you, mouthing the word "rich" when Sierra can't see.

"So what do I wear with it?" you ask, looking down at your jeans.

"Those look good," Molly says. "But you might get cold."

"You will *not* find any rental ski pants to match that jacket," Sierra says, pointing out the obvious. "So just wear your jeans. You look hot. And that's what matters!"

43

You know that you would be warmer wearing a snowsuit, but the jacket does look cool. And who knows, maybe you'll run into Mitch—or Zac—on the slopes. You think for a minute, then...

You decide to rent something warmer to wear. Go to 50.

You want to wear the jacket. Go to 52.

You race down the hall to Mitch's room, and knock on the door. A tall guy with buzz-cut short dark hair answers. "Hi," he says, smiling down at you. "Do I know you?"

"Oh, I'm a friend of Mitch's—is he here?" you ask, out of breath.

"Who is it?" Mitch says, coming around the door. When he sees you, his face lights up and he grins. "Hey, what's up?"

"I need, well, we need some help, in our room," you start to explain. "There's this bed thing...." You feel yourself getting all tongue-tied again.

"A bed thing?" Mitch's roommate says, laughing. "Maybe I can help!"

Mitch smiles. "I've got it, Travis," he says, then turns to you. "Lead the way."

Your face is so red at this point, you can hardly look at him as you walk back to your room. "It's called a Murphy bed," you say quietly. "It's, like, in the wall."

When you get to your room, the door is open—and Heather and Carrie are sitting on the Murphy bed! "We did it! There was a latch at the top that needed to be unhooked," Carrie explains.

"Hey, Mitch!" Heather says. "So cool to see you!"

"Well, I guess my work here is done," Mitch jokes, then he turns to you. "My friend Travis and I are about to go snowboarding—do you want to come with us?"

You look over at Heather and Carrie, who are busy pretending that they aren't listening to your conversation with Mitch. You were about to go skiing with them, and you know it would be rude to blow them off for a guy. But then again, you haven't seen Mitch in months—and you would love to catch up and hang out with him....

45

You decide to snowboard with Mitch. Go to 119.

You tell Mitch you'll see him later, and ski with the girls.
    Go to 120.

You go down the hall to search for Mrs. Bulow, and on your way, you run into Dan—Heather's crush.

"Hey," he says. "How's your room?"

"It's good, but we've got this problem. I'm looking for Mrs. Bulow; have you seen her?"

"No," he says, leaning against the wall, "but I'm glad I ran into you." He grins.

"Why?" you ask him, confused. "Is there something you needed?"

"Sort of," he says, and pushes his blond hair back from his face. "I just wanted to say that I still think you're really beautiful, and I still like you. I can't help it."

You're shocked. "I thought you had a crush on Heather," you say to him.

"Not really, I mean, honestly, I just started hanging out with her to get closer to you, and then she sort of started liking me, so..." He looks up at you. "Look, I feel like you've never really given me a chance. I know we had that one date—"

"I wouldn't call that a date!" you laugh,

remembering the day you went to a movie with him.

"Yeah, that movie *was* really terrible," Dan laughs. "But we still had fun, right?"

"I don't know—," you start to say, but he cuts you off.

"I'm ready to give it another chance"—he looks at you—"to give *us* another chance. If you are."

You remember, for a split second, how you used to feel about him, when you first met. What *did* go wrong between you two?

"Let's go skiing together, right now, just us. Let's hang out and see what happens," Dan says.

"But I think Heather might really like you," you argue.

"We'll deal with that later," Dan says. "Come on, please? Just give me one chance, then I'll leave you alone." He leans in close to you and touches your hair gently. It does seem like he's really into you—could it be true that he was just using Heather to get close to you?

You look back over your shoulder to be sure that no one has seen you two together, then you decide:

You should say no to Dan. Go to 186.
You want to join Dan for skiing. Go to 123.

You race back to your room, and throw on your ski clothes with a quick explanation to the girls. "Mitch asked me to meet him for skiing, so I'm going," you say as you dash out the door.

"Have fun," Sierra says in a sarcastic tone. You can tell that she doesn't like the idea—maybe he does have a girlfriend, but so what? It's not like it's a date or anything...right?

By the time you get downstairs, rent some skis, and get out to the chairlift, it looks like Mitch and Travis have been waiting awhile.

"What took so long?" Mitch says.

You don't know what to say, so you just shake your head. "Sorry."

"The line is a mile long now," Mitch sighs. "Let's just go to the T-bar," he says, huffing over through the snow with his skis. But when you get to the T-bar, it looks scary—you're supposed to balance your entire weight on this metal bar and sit just right so that it pulls you up the mountain.

"I don't know about this," you have to say. "What happens if I fall off?"

"It's not cool," Mitch says seriously. "They have to stop the whole thing until you can get on again. So don't fall off." He looks up to the front of the line impatiently.

"This line is long, too," Travis points out.

"I noticed," Mitch says. You had forgotten what a grump he could be sometimes. This is one side of Mitch that you haven't missed at all. Suddenly, you're wondering if maybe you should have just gone skiing with the girls.

"If you're not into this, I'll wait on the chairlift line with you," Travis says quietly. With his close-cut dark hair and deep brown eyes, he's handsome in an almost movie-star way.

You have missed Mitch, and you do want to spend time with him, but the T-bar is a little scary. Plus, it really seems like he's in an awful mood. But do you dare to ride the chairlift up with his friend—some guy you hardly know?

If you decide to brave the T-bar with Mitch, go to 55.
If you'd rather ride the chairlift with Travis, go to 57.

"I love this jacket," you tell Sierra. "But I think I might freeze my butt off."

"Yeah, sometimes you have to pick being warm over looking hot!" Sierra laughs.

"I'm going to rent a snowsuit. See you guys in a few minutes," you say. When you reach the lobby, you can already see the line for rentals—it's really long! Ugh. After you've been waiting for a few minutes, someone comes up behind you.

"Hey there," Zac says, shooting you a big metal grin. "Long line, huh?"

"Definitely makes me wish I had my own ski stuff," you say, watching other kids make their way out onto the slopes.

"I'm not a good enough skier to have my own stuff," Zac admits, walking forward as the line moves. "Actually, once I get my gear, I'm going over to take a ski lesson with that guy Bryce Karr—you know him?"

"That name sounds familiar," you say, racking your brain.

"He was in the Olympics a few years ago—he didn't win the gold medal, but he's still really amazing," Zac explains. "Hey, do you want to come and take the lesson with me? It's in half an hour. I think your friend Heather has signed up for it, too."

"I'm supposed to meet Molly and Sierra once I get my stuff," you say.

"Molly is a great skier," Zac says. "Are you sure you'll be able to keep up?"

"I don't know," you say. You don't want to be a drag.

"So come take this lesson with me instead," Zac says. "We can hang out, or whatever..." Suddenly, he starts getting all shy and silly.

You would like to hang out with Zac some more, but the slopes will be open for only a few more hours. If you take a lesson, you can kiss your chances of skiing with your friends goodbye, at least for the rest of the day. So it's cutie Zac and the ski lesson, or hanging out with your new friends. You look over at Zac and tell him:

51

"Okay, let's take that lesson." Go to 60.

"I'm going to skip it, thanks anyway." Go to 63.

"I think I will borrow your jacket, if it's okay with you," you tell Sierra.

"Of course! Borrow whatever you want," Sierra says.

"Okay, let's go!" Molly grabs your hand and pulls you out the door. You stop off at the rental desk to pick up a pair of skis, then meet the girls outside at the chairlift.

"Can we all get on at one time?" Sierra asks the guy running the chairlift.

"Well, I'm not supposed to let more than two on," he says, glancing around. "But okay—just don't tell anyone!"

The three of you squish onto the chair, and as it pulls you up, suddenly you're over the mountain, looking down on everyone on the snowy slopes. You're having a blast—and you feel so sophisticated in Sierra's silver jacket. "This is so fun. Thanks for letting me stay with you guys," you tell the girls.

Sierra puts her arm around your shoulders. "The

best ski trip ever!" she says. "Come on!" You all jump off the chairlift as it comes to a stop and make your way over to the head of an easy trail.

"We'll start slow, to warm up," Molly explains, pulling her ski goggles down over her eyes. She pushes off and goes down the slope, and you follow. But it's not as easy as it looks. You feel your left ski pulling out, so you try to bring your foot back in and—*whoops!*—your skis cross each other, and you go toppling over them!

"Nice one!" Sierra says, laughing. She slides to a stop and helps you get your ski boots hooked back on. "Okay?" she says when you're ready, and guides you down the mountain. It's amazing— the cold air in your face, the feeling of being fast and light as you move over the snow. The only problem is that your jeans are soaked from your fall—and they're sticking to your legs with an icy grip.

"Yuck, my jeans," you say, pointing them out to Molly when you two meet her at the bottom of the mountain.

"That looks uncomfortable," Molly says. "Do you

want to go change?" You think about it for a second. You do want to be warmer, but you don't want to miss a second of the fun. Plus, you love this silver jacket—do you want to have to give it up for a bulky snow coat?

54

You decide to rent something warmer. Go to 50.
You stay in the jeans and cool jacket. Go to 65.

"I'll try the T-bar," you tell Travis. "How bad can it be, right?" you laugh.

But Travis just gives you a smile. "You'll see," he warns. When it's finally your turn, you stand in the right spot with Mitch as the bar comes up fast behind you, hitting the back of your legs pretty hard. "See, it's not so bad," Mitch turns to you and says. You notice that's he's reaching down to hold on to the middle part of the bar, so you do too. But when you go to grab it, you lose your balance and suddenly fall forward—face-first into the snow! Luckily, the T-bar goes right over your head, but when you sit up, you see Travis on the next T-bar behind you coming up fast—with no way to stop!

"Skier down!" Travis yells, and the machine grinds to a halt. Everyone groans and you hear someone say, "Just get out of the way, already!" You go to scoot out of the way, but you're too afraid to stand up on your skis, so you're forced to scooch on your butt. When the guy running the T-bar sees that you're clear, he turns it back on and the skiers start moving again.

As Travis's bar goes over you, he says, "Head over to the beginner trail—I'll meet you there."

You look up and see that Mitch is going to take the T-bar all the way to the top—to a really difficult trail. You were looking forward to hanging out with him, but it seems like he doesn't feel the same way about you. What happened to the Mitch you used to know? Maybe he's just in a bad mood and you should give him another chance. You really want to show him that you're not a total klutz and that you can ski! You could get back on the T-bar when it stops, and make your way up there. Or you could stay where you are, on an easier trail, and meet Travis. You decide to:

Get back on the T-bar and head up to the harder slope.
Go to 67.

Stay where you are and meet Travis. Go to 69.

"Maybe the T-bar is a little much for me," you admit. "I'm going to go wait for the chairlift instead," you tell Mitch.

"I'll go with her," Travis says, and Mitch looks over at him with a smirk. "What?" Travis asks, looking right at Mitch. "You know I hate the T-bar."

"Do whatever you want," Mitch says, and turns his back to you both—obviously, he's not happy.

"Come on," Travis says, leading the way, and you two take your place at the end of the long line for the chairlift.

"So," you say, trying to make conversation with Travis, "does Mitch like going to school at Marshall?"

"I think he misses some stuff from his old school," Travis says, pushing the snow around with his boot. "I'm sure you already know this, but he used to have a crush on you."

"Really?" You try to act surprised.

"Yeah, when he first started at Marshall, he used to talk about you all the time," Travis goes on.

Even out here in the cold, you feel your cheeks start to turn slightly red, and you look away so that he can't see. "What kind of stuff did he say?" you can't help but ask.

"That you were cute," Travis says, moving forward with the line. "And he was right," he adds quietly.

You find yourself looking right into his dark eyes for a second before he glances away. "But then he started seeing this really popular girl and he stopped talking about you," Travis admits.

"So that's what's going on. I was wondering if maybe he was mad at me or something." The guy running the chairlift motions for you to step up. After you both sit, Travis leans across you to lock the bar into place, his hand brushing across your knee for a second.

"You okay?" he says, sitting back and taking off his hat. You're busy taking in his super-short dark hair, his intense eyes.... When he catches you staring at him, you quickly turn your head.

"Look at that!" you say, pointing to the top of the mountain where the chairlift is taking you. You can see the dark peak poking through the snow, and skiers all over the trails, zooming down.

"This is the best part of skiing, I think," Travis says. "I'm glad you didn't want to take that stupid T-bar."

"I know, right?" you agree. "We would have missed all this!"

"And I would have missed seeing it with you," Travis says quietly. The way he's looking at you, you can tell he's about to kiss you. The moment is beyond romantic, but are you ready to move on from Mitch—with his best friend?

If you want to kiss Travis, go to 72.
If you feel funny about kissing Mitch's best friend, go to 122.

You forgot your gloves, so you go back to the room to get them before making your way out to the "bunny trail" for the ski lesson. When you do get there, the lesson has already started. The first person you notice is Bryce Karr—he's tall and really tan, with blond curls poking out of his knit hat. "Hey, girlie," he says to you with a wink, "here for the ski lesson?"

All you can do is nod as you look around for your friends. You see Heather standing with a group of girls and go over to join her. "Hot enough for ya?" she jokes, motioning to Bryce.

"Beyond hot," you agree. "And also way too old for us!"

"Maybe for you," Heather says, and you both start giggling.

"Seriously, he was in the Olympics before we were born!" you point out.

"I know that, but check out his 'assistant,' would you?" You look over and see a really good-looking guy with dark hair pulled back in a ponytail, standing by Bryce.

"He's okay," you say, just as Zac sees you and waves.

"Hey!" he says, excited to see you. "Ready for the lesson?"

You can tell that Heather is annoyed that he's there. "I have a question for the instructor," she says, "I'll be right back." She scoots off toward Bryce.

"Listen," Zac says, sounding a little embarrassed. "I wanted to ask you something. If you don't have plans tonight, there's going to be karaoke in the lounge—all ages. I'm going, if you want to...." He trails off.

"Yeah, maybe," you say, just as Bryce asks everyone to line up in a row.

"Let's all try to point the tips of our skis together—make a triangle by turning your knees and ankles in," Bryce starts off.

Heather slides into place beside you and whispers, "Bryce and his assistant, Jon, have invited us to hang with them tonight! How awesome is that!" Her cheeks are flushed—and it's not from the cold.

You look up at Bryce as he walks by you, checking your ski position. "Good, let's just turn this one in a bit more." He adjusts your right ski. "This is how you put the brakes on, so you want to get it just right—otherwise, it's a total yard sale out there."

As his assistant comes up behind him, Heather says, "What's a yard sale?"

Jon laughs. "It's a wipeout where you lose all your stuff—you know, your skis, poles, gloves, everything all over the mountain. Looks like a yard sale or something."

"I get it," you laugh. Heather was right, Jon is actually adorable close up, with warm brown eyes and honey-colored skin. He moves over to Zac to help adjust his skis next, and Heather whispers to you, "So, you'll come out with us tonight, right?"

You look over at Zac for a second. He's a super sweet guy, and you know you'll have fun if you go to karaoke with him. But hanging out with Heather is always great, too—and who knows, maybe Jon has a friend for you?

You want to do karaoke with Zac. Go to 77.

You'd rather join Heather and hang out with Bryce and Jon. Go to 79.

When you're in your rented snowsuit, you head out to meet Molly and Sierra. As soon as you step outside, you're pretty happy that you rented something warm to wear.

"It's freezing out here!" you exclaim as the cold air hits your face.

"I know, they said it's one of the coldest days this year," Sierra says, pulling her knit hat down over her ears. "Brrrrr!"

Just then, something smacks you in the back with a wet thud. "Huh?" You spin around. "What was…"

Another snowball smacks Molly in the leg. "Hey!" she yells, and you all look over and spy a couple of guys hiding behind a snowbank, laughing at you.

"Hey, ladies!" one guy taunts as another snowball whizzes by your head.

"You missed!" Sierra yells. "Could they get any more immature?"

"I say we get 'em," Molly says, leaning over to pick up a handful of snow.

"I came here to ski, not play snowball fight with a bunch of little boys," Sierra says loudly. "How about you?"

"Well, there was this ski lesson that Zac mentioned, and it's starting right now," you say, looking over to where everyone is lining up for the lesson. You see Zac in line, and then notice that Heather is there, too.

"Come on, are you going to let these losers win?" Molly says, firing off a snowball. "Help me!"

If you want to get the boys back in a snowball fight, go to 81.

If you'd rather go join the ski lesson with your other friends, go to 60.

$\mathcal{E}$ven though you are a little cold, you decide to stay in your outfit. "Let's do another run, then," Sierra says, and you all ski over to the chairlift. As your chair goes up over the mountain, you can look down and see all of the skiers below you on the slopes. "Look at that guy," Molly points out. "Nice moves!"

"He's good," Sierra agrees. "And check her out." She points to a girl in a bright yellow snowsuit, zigzagging her way down the mountain.

"I have an idea!" Molly says, her eyes sparkling. "When we get to the top, let's do the trail that runs practically right under the chairlift—that way everyone coming up can check out our stuff!"

"That's a really hard trail," you say. "It's steep and looks icy."

"But those hot guys who were behind us in line would *have* to notice us if we skied down it," Sierra reasons.

As the chairlift carries you higher, you feel your wet jeans practically freezing onto your legs—

you're so cold, even your thighs are starting to feel numb! "You okay?" Molly asks. "Your teeth are chattering!"

"I might need to get off at the first stop and just ski down to the lodge to warm up," you say sadly.

"And miss your chance at hotdogging it down the slope in that amazing outfit?" Sierra says.

"Come on," Molly says. "There will be plenty of time to warm up later tonight—once we've met those cute boys!"

You're just too cold for the dangerous slope. Go to 84.
You decide to give the steep slope a try. Go to 86.

You have to ski uphill to get to the next stop for the T-bar—not an easy task—but you do it and finally get yourself up to the trail where Mitch is about to head down. "Hey, wait for me!" you yell over to him.

He's surprised to see you. "I thought you wiped out back there," he says, smiling. You're so glad to see that his mood has improved now that he's skiing.

"I did," you admit. "But I got back on and here I am, ready to go." You slide into position next to him and then look down the slope in front of you—and get dizzy! "Whoa, that's..."

"I know," Mitch says. "It's a black diamond trail called 'The Plunge.' I didn't know you were a good enough skier to go down this one." He's obviously impressed. So it kills you to have to set him straight.

"Actually..." You take another look down the mountain. "I'm, um..."

"Hey!" Someone slides up beside you—it's Zac!

"I thought I might run into you on the slopes—but not here!" He motions to the steep precipice.

"Yeah, we were just talking about that," you laugh.

"I already skied this one once and totally wiped out, so I'm headed over there"—he points—"to a slightly less crazy slope." Zac takes one look at your face and can tell you're terrified. "If you want to join me—," he starts to say, but Mitch cuts him off.

"No way. She's doing the black diamond trail with me, right?" You love the fact that Mitch is finally paying attention to you, but you're just not sure you can go down that dangerous slope. Mitch is looking at you so expectantly—do you dare to let him down? You take one more look at the skiers going down the black diamond trail and decide to…

Ski the hard slope with Mitch. Go to 74.
Ski the easy slope with Zac. Go to 89.

You ski carefully over to the beginner trail and wait for Travis. When he gets there, you expect him to make a joke about how you wiped out, but instead he quickly asks, "Are you okay?" He looks at you so sympathetically that you almost laugh.

"I'm fine—just a slightly bruised ego!"

Travis smiles. "I knew we should have skipped the T-bar. I hate that thing!"

There's something about the way he says "we" that makes you grin—it's like you're a couple or something. "Ready to tackle this trail?" he asks you.

"I guess so." You move into position next to him. "I just feel wobbly today."

"Here." Travis puts both his ski poles into one hand and holds out his other hand to you. "You just keep your eyes on the trail. I'll hold your hand on the way down, okay?"

Your mind instantly goes to Mitch—what would he think if he saw you holding hands with his best friend? Then you remember that he's been a jerk to you all day—and as far as you know, he's got a girlfriend.

"Hold your poles like this," Travis says, putting both of your ski poles into your left hand. He takes your right hand and holds it firmly. "You're gonna be great. Don't worry," he whispers as he pushes off from the top of the trail and pulls you with him. It definitely helps to have him there holding you up— even though you *still* almost fall a couple of times!

At the bottom, you see Heather waving, waiting for you. When she sees that Travis is with you, she makes a weird face. "He's a friend of Mitch's from Marshall," you explain, before she can even ask.

"Well," she says, "I was just looking for you to see if you wanted to sign up for a ski lesson—looks like you could use one!"

"With Bryce Karr?" Travis asks. "I hear he's great—he skied in the Olympics."

"And he's gorgeous." Heather giggles and nudges you—you want to joke with her, but you can tell she's making Travis feel totally uncomfortable.

"Guess I'm going to head out," he says to you. "If you decide that you need a ski lesson, just know that I'm available, too. I may not be an Olympic champ, but, well…you know where to find me," he says as he skis off.

"'Bye," Heather calls after him, then grabs your arm. "Are you going to do the lesson?" You can't help thinking about Mitch again—are you ready to totally give up on him? And even if you are ready, is it right to move on with his best friend? Maybe you should just take the ski lesson with Heather. Why does Travis have to be the nicest, cutest boy you've ever met? You don't know what to do!

71

You decide to let Travis give you a ski lesson. Go to 91.

You'd rather take a ski lesson with Heather. Go to 60.

$\mathcal{A}$s soon as you feel Travis's lips on yours, you know you made the right decision—he sends shivers down your spine. But in an instant, your mind is back on Mitch, and feeling guilty.

You pull away from him for a second. "I have to tell you something. Until today, I had a big crush on Mitch. And last year, something almost happened between us—," you start, but Travis cuts you off.

"Actually, I know all that. Boys talk, too, you know!" Travis explains. "What I'm trying to tell you is that Mitch has moved on, and I think you're ready to move on, too. Aren't you?" he asks, searching your face.

You look up and meet his gaze; the answer is clear. "I am ready," you admit. "I just hope he won't be mad at me."

"You let me deal with that," Travis says, putting his arm around your shoulders. "Right now, let's just ski and have fun, okay?" he asks as the chairlift starts to descend.

"Okay," you agree.

When you get off the chairlift, he holds your hand as you ski over to the slope. "Oh, and one more thing," he says, sticking his poles into the snow hard. "If I beat you to the bottom, you have to be my date to the movie at the lodge tonight." He grins at you and—*whoosh!*—he's gone.

You have to laugh as you start, slowly, down the mountain behind him. Even though you can't wait to see him at the bottom, this is one race you don't want to win!

END

"You think you're ready to do this?" Mitch asks from the top of the black diamond trail.

The trail is super steep, but you nod your head, and he gives you his classic grin. You can't help but smile back. Even if Mitch does have a girlfriend, there's still a chemistry between you two—you hope that you'll always be friends.

The two of you head down the trail next to each other, and you're doing great…at first! But as you build up speed, you feel unsure of yourself, and near the end of the trail, you wipe out, skidding on your butt as your skis pop off! Mitch slides to a stop, too.

"What happened there?" he says to you, still out of breath. He reaches down with one hand to help you up. But when you grab it, you pull down too hard, and he falls down—almost on top of you! He rolls over in the snow. "Very sneaky!" he says through a smirk.

"It was an accident," you say, tossing a handful of snow at him.

"Oh yeah?" He picks up some snow to throw at you, and before you know it, you're wrestling in the snow. Mitch finally pins you to the ground and leans over you, laughing so hard he can barely talk. "No more throwing snow!" he says. "Promise?"

"Yes!" you laugh, but as soon as he lets go of you, you grab a big handful of snow and shove it down the back of his jacket. "AHHHHHH!" he yells, hopping around, trying to get the snow out of his coat. That's when you notice a girl with long blond hair watching you two. She has her arms crossed over her chest and she doesn't look very happy.

"Hello, Mitch," she says in a voice that could freeze icicles.

"Oh, uh…," he says, the smile gone from his face. "I thought you weren't coming on the trip."

"Obviously," she says, staring at you.

"This is my girlfriend, Hannah," Mitch says to you quickly.

"Make that ex-girlfriend," Hannah snips as she turns on her snow boot and storms off. Mitch grabs his ski stuff to chase after her—forgetting that you're even there.

"Hannah, wait!" he yells, racing behind her.

Oh well, so much for "just being friends."

END

If you want to rethink skiing with Mitch, go back to 55.

When you get down to the lounge that night for karaoke, you realize you're late. "I thought maybe you weren't coming," Zac says with a scowl when you show up.

"Sorry, I..." You hesitate, trying to think up an excuse.

"Don't worry about it," Zac says, looking up at the stage, where a girl is about to sing a Madonna song. "I'm sure you're very busy."

"What's *that* supposed to mean?" you ask him.

"I don't know, you seem pretty popular. I've seen how guys act around you." He looks away from the stage for a second and meets your eyes. "I'm sure you think I'm just some kid who has a crush on you or something."

You sit stunned for a second, trying not to be distracted by the terrible warbling coming from the stage. "That's not how I feel," you tell Zac, and you mean it. He's probably the sweetest guy you've ever met—you don't care that he's younger than you, even if your friends do.

"So your friends haven't been giving you a hard time about hanging out with the 'brainiac'?" he scoffs.

"I can make up my own mind about people," you tell him quickly. "I don't really care what my friends have to say about it."

Zac just frowns and looks back up at the stage.

"Okay," the emcee says, taking the microphone when the girl finally finishes singing. "Who is our next victim—how about a duet? Do we have any takers?" He looks out over the audience. "Come on, I've got that song 'Baby, You Broke My Heart' all cued up and ready to roll...."

78 You look over at Zac, who is still sulking a little bit and won't look over at you. Maybe you should pull him up onstage to sing a duet with you—it could be hilarious, and put him in a better mood. Or would that be too much—does he need some time to cool down and just hang out?

You want to pull Zac up to sing a duet. Go to 94.

You'd rather wait it out and just watch karaoke for now. Go to 96.

"**I**'m so psyched that you decided to come and hang out with us tonight—and not with that Zac kid," Heather says as she puts on another coat of mascara. You sigh and look at her in the mirror.

"Lay off him—he's a sweet guy," you say.

"Whatever," Heather scoffs. "Can I use your lip gloss?" she says, and you pass it over to her. "We better hurry—Jon said to meet them in the lobby, like, five minutes ago," she says, sweeping the gloss over her lips and checking her hair one more time.

When you get down to the lobby, Bryce is there, and he's got a date—an older girl who you recognize from the ski rental shop. "Hey, this is my lady, Amanda," he says, introducing you. Jon is there, and he's brought a friend along—a big guy with curly hair and an adorable grin. "And this is my friend Aiden," Jon says, looking right at you. Could he be more obvious?

"So we were thinking that we'd go into town to this club I know," Bryce says. Then he adds, with a whisper, "The only problem is that we don't exactly have a ride, but I think I've got an idea...."

Jon lets out a little laugh. "Yeah, man, a classic idea!" His friend Aiden also laughs. You and Heather just look at each other.

"What's so funny?" Heather asks.

"You'll see" is all Bryce will say.

You're suddenly feeling worried—you're not supposed to leave the lodge without telling the chaperones, and you're obviously not supposed to leave with a group of guys! You turn to Heather and whisper, "I don't know about this; maybe I should just go and join Zac at the karaoke night...."

"Oh, come on," she says, "don't you want to have fun?"

What would be more fun tonight, doing karaoke with Zac or going dancing with Heather and these guys? You think for a second, then decide to:

Head over to karaoke and meet Zac. Go to 77.

Sneak into town with the guys. Go to 98.

"You're right," you tell Molly. "We need to even the score before we hit the slopes!"

"Come on, Sierra!" Molly says, grinning as she scoops up a handful of snow and packs it into a hard ball.

"Well, okay," Sierra says, quickly making a small snowball. She fires it at one boy's head. "Hey, no fair!" you hear a guy squeal. "No hitting in the face!"

"I think I got him," Sierra laughs as she packs another snowball. You crouch down and make a few snowballs, then fire them off fast.

A guy in a white hat peeks around the snowbank, and you shoot a snowball at him—and miss. "You're pretty good," he yells over to you, "but not fast enough!" And he pegs you in the leg.

"Hey," you shout after him as he ducks back behind the snowbank. "Did you see that guy, the one with the white hat?" you ask Sierra.

"Actually..." She starts to say something, then turns back to making a snowball. "Just look out for him—he goes to our school, and he's—" A snowball hits near her foot and she yells, "Watch it!" as she hurls one back.

You collect a few snowballs, the go around the snowbank and see your guy. You pelt him—fast—in the back with two before he can even turn around.

"What...," he says, and you slam him with another one before racing off.

"Got him!" you yell to the girls.

"Okay, truce, truce!" the guy says, waving a white hat over his head. "We surrender!" The guys come out from behind the snowbank with their hands up.

"Yes!" Molly says. "We killed you guys!" She gives one guy a high five, and it's clear to you that she and Sierra know them all from school.

"Hey, nice job," the guy with the white hat says to you. "I'm Alex." He takes his gloves off to shake your hand. "Man, your hands are warm!" he says, holding on to your hand for longer than he should. "I'm freezing—wanna go get a hot chocolate?"

Sierra overhears and looks over at you two talking with a scowl on her face. "Oh, actually, I was just about to go skiing with Sierra and Molly," you explain.

"One hot chocolate?" he says, giving you some

serious puppy-dog eyes. "I promise I won't keep you more than ten minutes. Besides, I think you owe me—you seriously damaged my pride in that snowball fight." He grins.

You look over at Sierra and Molly, who are ready to line up for the chairlift. They won't be too happy if you tell them to go on without you. Then again, this Alex guy is beyond cute—you'd like to go with him to the café. But what was Sierra trying to tell you about him? It didn't sound good. Do you dare to find out on your own?

You say yes to hot chocolate with Alex. Go to 100.
You'd rather ski with the girls. Go to 102.

"Sorry, guys," you tell Sierra and Molly, "but my legs are numb! I'm going to head down to the café."

"You poor thing," Molly says. "Well, watch out the window for us, and tell us how we look later, 'kay?" she says as the chairlift grinds to a halt at the first stop.

"Yeah, feel better," Sierra says, waving her glove at you as you carefully climb off and ski back down to the lodge. You pop off your skis and set them by the door, then go into the café and order a hot chocolate. While it's being made, you look around for somewhere to sit. The café is packed—lots of families with little kids in snowsuits, and tons of students from both your school and Marshall, but you don't see anyone you know.

"One hot chocolate," the guy behind the counter says, handing it to you. A couple gets up from one table, where you could sit by yourself if you want to, but maybe you should look around for someone to sit with? You *are* pretty tired, but it also might be a good chance to meet someone new....

If you want to sit alone, go to 106.

If you want to look for someone to sit with, go to 108.

"Okay, I guess one last run can't hurt, right?" You say to Molly and Sierra. "Even if my legs are numb!"

As the chairlift grinds to a halt, all three of you climb off and head over to the trail that runs right underneath it. "Wow, this is more steep than I thought," Molly admits, pulling her goggles down over her eyes.

"I think we can do it," Sierra says.

You can feel your teeth chattering, you're so cold. "I just hope I can feel my legs by the time we reach the bottom," you joke.

"Let's go!" Molly yells, pushing off with her poles. When she's a safe distance in front of you, you push off, too, and Sierra comes right behind you. In a second, you feel like you're going fifty miles an hour downhill. "Whooooooooooo!" you hear Molly yell from up ahead of you. And you do feel great—your hair flying out behind you, and wearing this awesome silver jacket. You look up to the chairlift going over your head and see two cute guys—one of them is using his cell phone to take a picture of you!

"Hey, boys!" you hear Sierra yell from behind you, and the guys start waving like crazy—Molly was right! Then, suddenly, your right ski catches on something and, before you know it, you're flipping down the mountain—you can't stop! When you finally reach the bottom, you're bruised and freezing, but all in one piece.

"Nice one!" you hear a guy yell from the chairlift, and laughter drifts down to you. *Ugh*.

As you gather up your poles and skis, your jeans are so wet and cold, they feel frozen to your body. "I think I better go inside," you mumble to Sierra and Molly. When you finally get up to the room, it takes you forever to peel off the soaked, icy jeans. Then you climb into bed and fall asleep.

〜

When you wake up, sunlight is streaming through the windows in your room—it's the next morning!

"You okay?" Sierra asks when she sees that you're awake.

"We tried to wake you up when we got back from the slopes, but you were out cold!" Molly says.

"And snoring!" Sierra adds. "You missed the best night ever—wait until you hear about the guys we met...," she starts. You're so bummed! How did you sleep through the whole thing? Maybe next time, you'll pick clothes that help you stay warm instead of an outfit that just makes you look hot!

END

If you want to wear something else for skiing, go back to 50.

"I think this trail is too hard for me," you tell Mitch. "Maybe after I warm up on the easier trail, I'll come back and meet you."

"Fine," Mitch says as he turns his back to you and heads down the trail.

"Let's go," you tell Zac, and head over to the easier trail with him. On your way, you ski by a group of girls giggling and talking to some boys from your school—obviously flirting and having fun—and it makes you think of Mitch. You look over at Zac for a second. You do like him, and he's really sweet, but there's something missing—that spark you feel whenever you're with Mitch.

"Ready?" Zac says when you both reach the top of the slope.

You decide to put the whole Mitch thing out of your mind and just have fun. "Let's go!" you yell as you push off with your poles.

When you're about halfway down the mountain, you hear something beside you—a loud *thump*—and look down to see Zac rolling down the mountain! "Zac!" you yell, just as he tumbles off the trail and into some fresh powder. You slant your skis to stop yourself, then go over to him.

"Are you okay?" you ask, but you can tell he's not.

"My ankle," he says, holding his leg, "I think it's hurt."

You can already hear a rescue snowmobile racing up the mountain to help. When the guy arrives, he jumps off to help Zac onto the back. "Sorry, there isn't enough room for you, but we can meet you down at the infirmary," he tells you.

"That's okay," Zac says, looking more concerned for you than for himself. "You should keep skiing and have fun. I'll see you later."

"Are you sure you're going to be okay?" you ask him.

"Don't worry about it." Zac gives you a weak smile as the snowmobile races off down the mountain. You had wanted to meet back up with Mitch later and ski with him. But can you leave Zac all by himself in the infirmary?

You decide to ski down to the infirmary with Zac. Go to 110.

You'd rather go back and ski with Mitch. Go to 74.

When you get a text message from Travis that night on your phone, you're so happy, you practically jump up and down.

It only asks if you want to meet for a ski lesson tomorrow, but that's enough. You immediately accept. You can hardly wait!

⌒〜⌒

The next morning, you show up early to meet him, and he's already there. "You ready?" He grins at you, and you two ski over to the bunny trail, where he takes you through some basics. Every time he touches you, a shiver goes up your spine.

"I think we can hit an actual trail now," he says, pulling a knit cap down over his short, dark hair. "Come on." He takes your gloved hand in his and leads you over to the chairlift. When you get to the top of the trail, Travis says, "Try to remember everything I just showed you, okay? Keep your knees bent, stay low," he reminds you.

"I've got it," you say, using your poles to push off. As you start down the trail, you're trying hard to keep everything Travis taught you in mind—and it's working! Before you know it, you're at the bottom of the trail—and you didn't wipe out once!

"I did it!" you shout to Travis as he slides to a stop right next to you.

"I know, you did great!" he says, and moves to grab you in a hug—but your skis and his get in the way. "Here," he says, popping his skis off. He comes over to you and wraps his arms around you. "I'm proud of you—really," he says quietly in your ear. When he steps back, he gives you a serious look.

"The only thing left to discuss is the payment," he says.

"What payment?" you ask him, confused.

"For the lesson," he jokes. "I may not be an Olympic champ, but I still have to charge you for my time."

"Of course," you joke back. "So what do I owe you?"

"I think…"—he leans in close to you—"three Eskimo kisses sounds about right."

"It's a bargain," you say, blushing as he moves

his face closer to yours. When your noses touch, you look up into his eyes and smile, just as you feel his lips touch yours. Who knew learning to ski could be so much fun?

END

You reach over and grab Zac's hand. "Come on!" you say, pulling him up to the stage before he can say no.

"I can't sing," he whispers to you.

"So?" you tell him. "That's what karaoke is all about!"

You turn to the emcee and say, "We'll do it!"

"Great, two new victims." He hands you each a microphone, points down at the monitor, and says, "Good luck!" as he walks off the stage.

"I don't know this song!" you whisper to Zac.

"I don't, either!" he whispers back, just as words start crossing the monitor—and the lyrics are so embarrassing!

"Oh baby, I can't let you go...," you try to sing along with the music.

"Ohhhhh, you broke my..." Zac pauses to look at the monitor for a second. "Uh, my heart," he sings, and everyone laughs.

The next line is yours: "I didn't mean to do you wrong...baby," you sing, laughing.

"Ohhhhhh, baby...," Zac starts. "Wait, that's *your* line!" he says, pointing at you. Pretty soon, everyone in the audience is laughing so hard, you can't even remember what you're supposed to be singing. So you and Zac just sing every line together, making them laugh more. When the song finally ends, there's tons of clapping—some people even stand up to cheer for you both!

"Kiss her!" someone yells out, and suddenly the crowd is chanting, "Kiss, kiss, kiss, kiss!"

Zac looks at you, smiling, "I think we need to give our fans what they want," he says quietly.

"I agree," you say, leaning in. When his lips touch yours, the audience goes crazy cheering.

"Encore!" someone yells.

"Uh, maybe later," Zac says into the microphone. He grins at you as he takes your hand and leads you offstage. Not every guy is sweet enough to put up with the craziness of a spontaneous karaoke duet, but Zac is. He's adorable! That's the last time you judge anyone based on just their age!

END

"We'll do it!" you hear someone say, and a guy goes up to the stage holding a girl's hand. They take the microphones and start singing a terrible duet about heartbreak and getting dumped.

"You'd never want to do something like that with me," Zac says, motioning to the people onstage. "You'd be too embarrassed to be seen with some nerd." He slumps down in his seat.

"That's not true," you say.

"Look"—he turns to you—"I might as well just tell you. I heard what you and your friends were saying about me; one of my friends overheard you."

"I don't know what you're talking about," you tell him, but your mind goes back to some of the things that Heather had been saying. Who could have overheard her?

"About how I'm just some little kid, some super-brain….Why did you even agree to meet me here tonight? Just to make fun of me?" he asks.

You can tell he's really angry, and you feel terrible. "Zac, I—," you start to say, but he cuts you off.

"Forget it," he says. "I'm out of here." He stands up and pushes his chair into the table hard before leaving the lounge. You feel bad that he heard you and your friends were talking about him, but seriously...maybe he is too immature for you after all!

END

Want to sing with Zac instead of fight with him?
Go back to 94.

"Here's the idea," Bryce says, leading you all out into the parking lot. "We'll just borrow the lodge's van for the night—they'll never notice that it's gone."

"Yeah, and besides, we *are* lodge employees, so we should be allowed to use it, right?" Jon adds.

"That's what I'm thinking," Bryce whispers. He leads the way through the dark parking lot over to a van that has MT. FROST SKI LODGE painted on the side of it. He opens the sliding door on the side. "Climb in," he says to you and Heather.

She climbs up into a seat, and you join her. Aiden scoots in beside you. Bryce goes around to the driver's seat and gets in while Amanda takes the passenger seat next to him. "Now for the tricky part," Jon says, climbing into the back of the van and closing the door. "You sure you've got this?"

"Yeah, man, no prob," Bryce says as he reaches under the steering wheel.

"What are you doing?" Heather asks.

"Well, see, we don't *exactly* have the keys," Bryce

after being hit hard with snow bullets! You've got quite an arm; do you play softball or something?" he flirts.

"Stop it." You smile. "I didn't hit you that hard...did I?"

"I think I'll live," he says, rubbing his shoulder. You love the way his dimples show up when he laughs.

You look down into your hot chocolate for a second, wondering if you should just clear the air and ask him about Sierra—how he knows her, and why she seems to dislike him so much. But you're having so much fun just sitting here, getting to know him, that you almost don't want to ruin it.

Suddenly you realize that there's an awkward silence between you—should you ask him about Sierra or just ignore it and make small talk?

You decide to ask him about what Sierra said. Go to 176.

You'd rather just ignore it. Go to 178.

"Sorry, I'm going to ski with my friends," you tell Alex.

"Ouch," one of his friends says, laughing, but Alex just shoots you a grin.

"Maybe I'll see you later?" he says as you walk away. You give him a little wave as you turn to catch up with Molly and Sierra.

"Good thing you didn't go with him," Sierra whispers to you. "He's a real jerk."

"Really?" you ask her. "He seems so sweet."

"Who seems sweet?" Molly asks, tuning in to the conversation.

"No one," Sierra says fast. "Hey, let's go get in line!"

That night, after you've been skiing for hours, Sierra and Molly eat dinner with you, then join a bunch of other students from Marshall at the lodge fire. As soon as you settle into a comfy couch and enjoy the warmth of the fire, Sierra says, "You know what we need? Popcorn!"

"I'll go to the kitchen and see if I can find some," you volunteer. You head down the long hallway, back to the kitchen, but it looks like no one is around. It's kind of scary in there after dark, and most of the lights are out. "Hello?" you say, hearing your voice echo in the empty dining hall.

"Hey," someone says, and you practically jump.

"Oh, Alex! You scared me!" you say. He looks different out of his ski clothes—tall and thin in baggy jeans and a T-shirt.

"I was just looking for a snack," he says, grinning. "What are you up to?"

"Popcorn. We're sitting by the lodge fire, and Sierra…" You stop yourself, suddenly remembering what Sierra said about him.

"Yeah, so you and Sierra are friends, huh?" he asks, looking down for a second.

"She say anything about me?"

"Uh…" You don't know how to answer him, so finally you just tell the truth. "Yeah, she did."

Alex nods and looks glum. "It was a bad breakup, what can I say? I tried to be as nice as I could," he explains. "But I guess it's never easy. So I look like the bad guy, you know?"

"Wait, you and Sierra used to go out?" you ask him. That would explain everything!

"Yeah, she didn't tell you? We dated for two years, then when we started high school, I don't know, things changed," he goes on. "I think she still hates me, but you know what? I'm not a bad guy. Things just didn't work out."

You just nod. So *that's* why Sierra didn't want you to hang out with him.

"The truth is, since we broke up, I haven't even looked at another girl. Until today...," he says, glancing up at you.

You don't know what to say, so you just smile, and he smiles back, a dimple showing in one cheek in the cutest way.

"So if I help you find the popcorn, will you promise to be on my team tomorrow for the rematch snowball fight?" Alex says.

"And help you guys win? I don't think so," you joke.

"Well, then, will you at least sit with me at the lodge fire tonight?" he asks, and you can tell he's being totally sincere.

You know that Sierra won't like it, but it sounds like it's time for her to get over her ex and move on. "Sure," you tell him, blushing.

"Then I guess we better find that popcorn," he says, opening a big cabinet. Who would have ever guessed that one silly snowball fight could lead to a date with a super-cute guy?

END

You sit by the window, alone, and drink your hot chocolate, but it doesn't do a lot to warm you up. When you're done, you go upstairs to change, but once you get the wet, frozen jeans off, you're so tired, you just collapse into bed.

When you wake up, it's dark outside, and Sierra and Molly are just getting back from the slopes. "Are you okay?" Sierra asks, slipping out of her snowsuit.

"Ugh," you moan. Your throat feels all scratchy and your nose is running like crazy. "I think I'm sick."

"Oh no, I guess that means no karaoke for you," Molly says, pulling out a hot outfit for the night.

"And probably no skiing tomorrow, either," Sierra adds with a pout.

"We'll bring you back some soup," Molly says as both girls go into the bathroom to do their makeup.

You get out of bed to grab a tissue and see your wet jeans and Sierra's silver jacket lying on the floor. "Ugh," you say again, walking over to the mirror on wobbly legs. When you look at yourself, though, you feel even worse. You may have looked hot on the slopes in that silver jacket, but right now you're paying the price!

END

Want to change that ski outfit? Go back to 50.

You look around and finally see a really adorable guy with spiky dark hair whom you recognize from the chairlift. Sierra and Molly introduced you to him, but he was in a group of guys, so you don't really know him. You walk over to his table. "Hi," you say softly, and he looks up.

"Hey, you're Sierra's friend, right?" he says. "I'm Alex. You wanna sit?" He motions to the empty chair.

"Thanks," you say, wrapping your hands around your hot chocolate mug. "It sounds silly, but I didn't realize it was going to be this cold here—I'm freezing!"

"Really? You looked great out there—that jacket is awesome."

"Oh this?" You look down at Sierra's silver coat. "Actually, it's not mine. And I'm totally freezing because I wanted to wear it."

"Well, it does look good on you," Alex says, and gives you a dimpled grin.

"I just came in to warm up, then I'm going back out to ski with my friends," you tell him.

"I have a better idea," he says. "Why don't you change into something warmer and we'll go sledding—it's about to get dark out, and the night sledding is amazing!"

Your only option for warmer clothes is renting one of the hideous snowsuits from the lodge— they're big, bulky, and totally unflattering. But you're so cold, there's no way you can go sledding—especially at night—in what you're wearing. Do you dare to hang out with this cutie in a big goofy snowsuit? Or should you tell him you're not in the mood to go sledding?

109

If you decide to join Alex for night sledding, go to 115.

If you're too embarrassed to wear a snowsuit in front of him, go to 117.

There's no way you can go ski with Mitch now—checking in on Zac and making sure he's okay is the right thing to do. You make your way down to the infirmary and start looking for him. When you find him, his face totally lights up.

"What are you doing here? You didn't have to come," he says, but you can tell he's psyched that you did.

"So what's the diagnosis?" you say, looking down at his swollen ankle.

"Just sprained. They're going to wrap it up. And I'll have crutches," he explains.

The nurse comes by. "It's going to be a couple of hours before the doctor can get here to look at your ankle," she says. "Do you want me to get you a book or a magazine? We have some games over here...." She points to a pile of old board games. You hear Zac let out a sigh.

"Hey, let's play Scrabble!" you say, and quickly set up the board on his bed, pulling a chair over for yourself. Before you know it, an hour has passed and Zac has beaten you—badly—at the game.

"The least you could do is let me win," you tease him. "I mean, I am taking time out from the slopes to hang with you!"

Out the window, you can see that the sun is going down behind the snowy mountain. No more skiing for you today, but you don't mind—you're having a great time hanging out with Zac—he's so smart, and super funny, time just flies by when you're with him.

The doctor finally shows up and sets Zac's ankle. "Obviously, no skiing tomorrow," he adds when he's done wrapping it in a bandage.

"That's okay," you tell Zac. "I hear they have a whole computer room in the lodge stocked with video games." But he doesn't look too happy.

"I was looking forward to hanging out with you," he admits. "Now I'm going to be stuck in the lodge all day while you're on the slopes."

You love that Zac isn't scared to tell you how he feels about you. For a guy who's a year younger, he's very mature! "Look," you tell him, "Why don't I ski for half the day, and spend the other half with you?"

His face lights up. "You'd do that for me? But wait—do I have to let you win?" he asks, smiling.

"No way, I want a fair rematch," you tell him.

"But if I do win, it might encourage me to spend less time on the slopes and more time with you. You take his hand in yours and look up at him.

"You've got yourself a deal," he says, grinning. And suddenly, you feel those sparks you thought were missing. Who needs skiing, anyway, when you can hang out with your new boyfriend all day?

END

"I think I need someone to get out and push the van," Bryce says, turning to Aiden and Jon. "That will help get it started."

The guys get out and go around to the back of the van as you scoot over by Heather. "This is crazy," you whisper to her.

"And fun!" she says back.

The van starts moving, and Bryce leans down under the steering wheel, messing with the wires again. "Uh, babe," Amanda says, reaching over for the wheel. "Look out—guys, stop pushing!" she yells as Bryce pops his head up and grabs the wheel.

Too late! The van tips down into a ditch at the edge of the parking lot with a loud *THUMP*, and you and Heather are almost thrown out of your seats.

"Uh-oh," you hear Bryce say, just as an ear-piercing beeping starts up—the van's alarm is going off!

"Let's get out of here!" Heather yells, trying to

open the sliding door on the side of the van. When you get outside, you can see that Jon and Aiden are already halfway across the parking lot, running. You grab Heather's hand and start off after them. But before you can get even a few steps, you see some figures coming toward you in the dark—it's the lodge director, and he's got Mrs. Bulow with him!

"What on earth?" Mrs. Bulow starts to say.

The director just looks at the van and shakes his head. "It's not the first time for these guys," he says, looking over at Bryce and Amanda. "You two, in my office, now," he orders.

"Girls, I can't believe you would help someone steal a car!" Mrs. Bulow says.

"We weren't helping," Heather starts to explain.

But Mrs. Bulow puts her hand up. "No excuses! Let's go inside and call your parents to come and get you—you're both going home, and possibly facing a suspension from school as well." As she leads the way back into the lodge, you take one look back at the van, stuck in the ditch. Maybe you should have gone to karaoke instead!

END

Want to try this night over again? Go back to 98.

When you show up to meet Alex for sledding, you're so embarrassed—the only snowsuit they had left at the rental shop was two sizes too big— and in bright orange!

"Wow," Alex says when he sees you. "That looks, um, warm." He grins at you and pulls a hat down over his spiky hair.

"Please don't say anything," you beg him. "It was the last one they had."

"I can see why," Alex jokes. "Seriously, though, as long as you're warm, that's all that counts." He picks up the toboggan and leads you over to the side of the bunny trail, where a long, slow hill descends in front of you.

"Hey, this is perfect for sledding," you say, noticing that the outside lights are snapping on as the sun goes down.

"Even better for *night* sledding," Alex says, putting the sled down. He climbs on and motions to you to join him.

"On the same sled?" you ask.

Alex nods. "Come on."

You sit down in front of him on the sled and he goes to put his arms around you. "I don't really like small girls anyhow," he jokes, struggling to get his arms around your puffy snowsuit. You glare at him over your shoulder, but suddenly the sled moves and you're racing down the hill. "Whoo-hoooo!" Alex hoots close to your ear, and holds your waist tighter. You love the way his strong arms feel around you as the sled skids to a stop.

"That was great, let's do it again!" you cheer.

"Now for the hard part," Alex says, standing and pointing up the hill.

"We have to walk back up?" you ask.

"Yup. And I think I need something to fortify me," he says, and before you can say anything he leans in for a quick kiss, touching your lips softly.

When he pulls away, he looks into your eyes for a second and pushes your hair back from your face. "I think I can safely say that you are the first girl in a giant orange snowsuit that I have ever kissed," Alex laughs, taking your hand and leading you back up the hill. And you think you can safely say that night sledding is your new favorite sport!

END

That night, you feel like you still can't get warm, so you bring a big blanket down to the lodge fire and curl up under it. Everyone around you is chatting, eating popcorn, and having fun talking about the day out on the slopes—except for you. You're still too bummed that you wore your jeans skiing, and that you were too embarrassed to go sledding with that adorable guy Alex when he asked you. You've decided that tomorrow morning you're going straight to the rental shop to get a snowsuit—no matter what it looks like. You're not about to ruin your whole trip over some fashion trauma! Who cares what you look like on the slopes—you came to have fun!

"Hey, what are you thinking about?" you hear someone say, pulling you from your thoughts. It's Alex, looking so good in a dark sweater that matches his eyes.

"Oh, I was just…," you start to say.

"You're still cold?" he asks, sitting next to you and taking your hand in his.

"A little bit," you admit shyly. "Hey, I thought you were going night sledding?"

"I was, but the girl I wanted to go with blew me off." He grins at you.

"I'm sorry, honestly, I was just thinking about that," you tell him. "If you want to know the truth, I just didn't want you to see me in a big dorky rental snowsuit." You look down at your blanket, too embarrassed to look at him.

"Why? You're so cute, who would even notice what you're wearing?" he asks softly. "So, tomorrow night?"

"You're giving me a second chance?" You smile.

"As many chances as it takes," he says, putting his arm around your shoulders. You smile and curl up under your blanket. For the first time all day, you finally feel toasty warm!

END

$\mathcal{W}$hen you meet the guys down at the rental shop, you can't believe how lucky you are! Mitch looks amazing in his blue snowboarding jacket that matches his eyes, and his friend Travis isn't bad-looking either, with his super-short buzz cut and cool sunglasses.

"Hey, guys," you say loudly, and wave—you want all the girls in the shop to know that these hot guys are with you!

"You know what size board you need?" Travis says, looking over at you.

"I bet the Burton Fifty-six would work," Mitch says.

"I don't know, a lot of girls like to use a kid's board—softer flex, easier to trick on...."

You look at the two of them like they are speaking some foreign language.

"What do you usually use?" Mitch asks you. "You *have* snowboarded before, right?"

You answer him honestly and say:

"Yes, I've snowboarded before." Go to 124.

"No, I've never snowboarded." Go to 126.

When you get down to the rental shop with Heather, you're still a tiny bit bummed that you turned Mitch down. Oh well, maybe you'll get a chance to see him later, and you know better than to choose a guy over your friends!

"Hello, ladies," a guy behind you says to Heather. "What's your poison today?"

"Huh?" Heather looks at him blankly.

"He means are you skiing or snowboarding," the guy's friend says.

"Oh, we're skiing," Heather says. "What about you guys?"

"I'm snowboarding," the redheaded guy says, "but my wimpy friend here is skiing. You want to go ski with these girls?" he teases.

"I wouldn't mind," the blond-haired guy says. "Hi, I'm Jim, and you'll have to excuse my friend here, he doesn't get out much."

"Well, you can join us if you want to. We're just renting some ski clothes, then we're going to hit the slopes," Heather says.

You're next in line, and the girl behind the counter says, "What size are you? Shoe size, too, if you need boots."

And you're suddenly horrified—you don't want to say your size in front of these cute guys! You're so embarrassed!

You make up an excuse to step out of line. Go to 128.

You decide to just say it—you have to get your ski stuff! Go to 130.

"I'm sorry, I just can't," you tell Travis, and he backs away from you.

"That's okay," he says. "I get it."

"It's just that I...," you start to explain, but Travis puts his hand up. "Don't worry about it, I'll get out of your way once we're off the chairlift." He looks so glum.

When the lift stops, you hop off and head over to meet Mitch, and Travis heads for another trail without saying anything to you.

Go to 74.

"Okay," you hear yourself say—and can hardly believe you're going to do it! "Just let me grab my stuff and I'll meet you downstairs." You can't really feel too bad about it, after all, he *did* like you first—even Heather knows that!

When you get back to the room to grab your coat, Heather gives you a confused look. "Where's Mrs. Bulow?" she asks you. "You couldn't find her?"

"Oh...right," you start to say. You forgot all about the bed, and trying to find Mrs. Bulow.

"Where are you going—outside?" Carrie asks, pointing at your jacket.

123

"Actually..." You think fast—what can you tell them? Do you tell the truth, that you're going to meet Dan, or make something up?

You decide to make something up. Go to 162.
You want to tell Heather the truth. Go to 135.

"I know how to snowboard," you tell Mitch, but inside you're secretly hoping that you're good enough to keep up with him and Travis. After you pick up your rental board, the three of you head over to the chairlift. When it's your turn to get on the chair, Mitch steps up beside you, leaving Travis behind. This will be the first time you've been alone with Mitch in months, and you can feel your heart start to beat fast!

"I'm glad you decided to come with us," Mitch says. "I know you had plans with your friends and everything...." He looks down, and his brown hair falls over his eyes.

You're glad, too, but you don't know what else to say, so instead you just point out the skiers on the slopes below you. "I love the chairlift—this is my favorite part. Just being up here, looking out over the mountain and everything..." You feel like you're rambling.

"Yeah, I know what you mean," Mitch says, catching your eye. When it's time to jump off the chairlift, you silently hope that you can get your back foot into your board and not look like a total amateur—and you do it on the first try! "Nice," Mitch says, noticing. "That's not easy—you really have snowboarded before."

When you reach the snowboarding trail, he asks, "You want to lead?"

"Sure," you say. But once you get started, you wish he had gone first, so that you wouldn't feel his eyes on your back, watching your every move. You try to build up some confidence as you make smooth S-curves down the mountain, and you're careful not to grind too much—you know how annoying it is to board behind someone who's totally chewed up the snow.

When you reach the bottom, Mitch slides up beside you. "You're really good!" he says, grinning, and you can tell he's impressed. "Hey, let's race the next run."

You want to say yes—and you're pretty sure you can keep up with him—but do you really want to race against your crush? What if you win, and he's a sore loser? Or worse, what if you totally wipe out and make a fool of yourself?

125

You say yes to the race with Mitch. Go to 137.
You'd rather not race against your crush. Go to 139.

"**A**ctually," you have to admit, "I've never snowboarded before."

"Oh great," Mitch says. "You're just going to slow us down then." He looks angry, and you're so hurt. You thought he wanted to hang out with you!

"I can help you," Travis says. "Let's rent a board and I'll give you a quick lesson," he says. Your eyes meet his for a second, and you feel your face getting warm. Why is he being so nice to you?

"I don't know," you say, "I don't want to keep you guys from having fun. My friend was telling me about this ski lesson that she was going to take, so maybe I'll just rent some skis and go join her," you tell him.

"It's not a big deal," Travis says, shrugging. "Really, don't listen to him," he adds in a whisper. "Everyone has to learn sometime, right? Why not now?" You're about to say something back to Travis when Mitch cuts in.

"Come on, if you're going, let's do it. I don't want to miss out on any more slope time," he says.

You look from Mitch to Travis. What is going on here? You wanted to spend time with Mitch, but he's being a real jerk, and Travis is being so sweet. Taking a lesson from him would probably be a lot of fun, and you do want to get to know him better. But he's your crush's best friend! You feel really confused. Maybe this whole snowboarding thing is just a recipe for disaster? Maybe you should just forget these two and go join Heather at the lodge ski lesson?

If you decide to say goodbye to the guys and head to the ski lesson, go to 60.

If you'd rather stay with them and snowboard, go to 141.

"Oh, I...um...have to go to the bathroom," you say suddenly, and dash out of the rental shop.

"Hey, wait!" Heather yells after you, but you keep going. You just couldn't say your size in front of those guys—it's too embarrassing! After a few minutes in the bathroom, you go back into the shop, but your friends have already picked up their stuff and gone. You get back into the line—which is now really long—and call Heather on her cell.

"Where are you guys?" you ask her.

"We're waiting for you, outside—what's the holdup?"

"I'm back in the line to get my stuff, and it looks like it's going to be a while," you admit.

"Well, I guess we'll go to the chairlift. Call me when you're ready to ski and we'll look for you," Heather says, and hangs up.

What a bummer. After what feels like forever, you finally get to the front of the line. "Size, shoe size, too," the girl behind the counter says, and this time you tell her. "Yeah, actually, we're out of that size. Here, try these," she says, pushing a pair of ski boots across the counter to you.

"These are two sizes too small," you tell her.

"Sorry, that's all we've got left," she says, and turns to help the next person. You go to try on the boots and your feet are so squished, there's no way you can wear them. And without ski boots, there are no skis—and no skiing! There goes your chance to ski with the cute boys—or to ski at all!—*argh*!

END

If you want to rewind your trip to the ski rental shop, go back to 120.

ou tell the girl your size. If Jim and his friend notice, they don't say anything, and you secretly breathe a sigh of relief! The girl behind the counter hands you your stuff just as Jim says, "So, seriously, can I meet you guys and ski with you?" You turn to look at him. He's got a bit of a bad-boy look, with short blond hair and a devilish smirk.

"Yeah, sure," you tell him, and look over at Heather to see what she'll say.

"Fine with me"—she grins—"I just hope you can keep up."

"That's a challenge I can't pass up," Jim's friend says. "Forget snowboarding, I'm coming, too."

You and Heather exchange a quick smile. So far this ski trip is turning out pretty great! "We have to go change, but we'll meet you guys out at the chair-lift," Heather tells them as you walk off. When you're out of earshot, you both start giggling. Then, as you head down the hallway to your room, you run into some of Heather's friends.

"Hey, Jenny!" Heather gives one girl a big hug.

"So cool to run into you—we just met some guys from your school!"

"Oh yeah, who?" the other girl asks.

"One guy named Jim, and a friend of his," you offer.

"Uh-oh," Jenny says. "Did the other guy have red hair, freckles?"

"Yes," Heather says quickly, "why, bad news?"

Jenny leans in. "They kinda have a reputation at school for being players."

"Oh no—we told them we'd meet them!" you say.

"Well, there is that ski lesson… we could go and do that instead," Heather points out. "We could just tell the guys we forgot that we'd signed up for it. "

"Better hurry," Jenny says, walking away with her friends. "That class starts in five minutes!"

Heather looks over at you. "What should we do?"

"They didn't *seem* like jerks," you say, "but maybe we should trust your friend?"

You want to meet the boys and decide for yourself.

Go to 145.

You'd rather just take the ski lesson. Go to 60.

$\mathcal{M}$rs. Bulow explains that there's a small clasp at the top of the Murphy bed that holds it closed. "Here, you just undo this," she says, opening the clasp, "and the bed comes right down." She pulls the handle and a bed folds out.

"Thank you so much," Heather says.

"Please remember, girls, that I'm here to help you out with any problems, okay?" Mrs. Bulow says. You're glad she's the head chaperone on the trip because she's always so nice. "Now you better hurry or you'll be late for Bryce Karr's first lesson of the day," she adds with a smile.

"Who's Bryce Karr?" Carrie asks.

"You don't know who Bryce Karr is?" Mrs. Bulow looks surprised. "He's a former Olympic champ, and now he teaches lessons here. I thought for sure all you girls would be signed up by now...," she says.

"Why? Do you think we need a ski lesson that badly?" you ask her with a laugh.

"No, because Mr. Karr is so...well, let's just say he's very, very handsome." Mrs. Bulow blushes.

Could it be that your teacher has a crush?

"Let's go!" Heather says, grabbing her coat.

Carrie quickly looks over her ski schedule. "Class starts in fifteen minutes!"

"'Bye, Mrs. Bulow," you turn and say as you race down the hall. But as you round the corner, you run right into…Mitch!

"Hey, slow down!" he says, laughing and catching you by your shoulders. "What's up?" He grins, and you feel your heart start to race.

"Um, uh, we're…well…" Your brain feels all scrambled. Why does he always have this effect on you?

"If you're not doing anything, besides racing in the hallways, do you want to come snowboarding with my friend and me?" He motions to the dark-haired guy standing next to him. You look over at your friends for a second—should you take the lesson with them or hang out with Mitch?

133

_____ ℓ _____

You decide to take the ski lesson. Go to 60.

You'd rather change plans and snowboard with Mitch.

Go to 119.

"Here you go," you tell Jim's friend, Henry, as you push him in front of you. "Why don't you ride up with your friend and I'll go with Heather."

"We'll meet you guys up there," Heather says cheerfully.

As soon as the guys are on the chairlift, you turn to Heather and whisper. "Let's head over to the ski lesson and ditch these guys—I'm getting a bad vibe from them."

"Me too!" Heather exclaims. "When you weren't looking, that Henry guy tried to kiss me!"

"Ewwww, creep!" you say as you two step out of the line and head over to the ski lesson.

"I forgot my gloves, I'm going to run to the lodge first, then I'll meet you there," you tell her. You hope Jim and Henry won't be too upset when they find out you totally stood them up!

Go to 60.

134

"Honestly?" you say, turning to face Heather. "I ran into Dan in the hallway and he asked me to go skiing with him."

"What do you mean, like a date or something?" Heather looks crushed.

"He said he still likes me and wants to hang out with me," you admit, grabbing your gloves and hat.

"But…he likes me!" Heather says. "And I like him, too. How could you do this to me?"

You just look at her for a second. She has been kind of mean to you this entire trip, but maybe you're just lashing out at her—maybe you don't really even like Dan that much.

"He told me he was just using you to get close to me," you tell her.

"What!?" Heather screams. "You've got to be kidding me!" She picks up her duffel bag and throws it against the wall, clothes flying everywhere. Then she sits on the bed and starts crying. "Why would he do this to me?" she says, and Carrie sits beside her.

"Look, just because Dan is a jerk, that doesn't mean you guys have to fight over him," Carrie points out. "Maybe neither one of you should date this guy. I mean, listen to the stuff he's saying—using one friend to get to another? That's just plain creepy."

You have to admit that Carrie is right. You sit on the other bed to think for a second. It's flattering that Dan is so into you, but do you really want to do this?

If you decide to meet Dan, go to 147.

If you'd rather blow him off and patch up your friendship, go to 149.

"Race...okay, why not?" you tell Mitch as you two line up at the top of the slope.

"On three," he says, and counts off, "one, two..." He pushes off.

"Hey, no fair!" You race after him. He's ahead of you, but you can tell he's boarding too fast and tight. You loosen up your S-curves and make a big loop around him, taking the lead. When you reach the bottom, you pretty much tie.

"I would have won—if you hadn't cheated," you say, catching your breath.

"Cheating? Me?" Mitch smiles at you. "Don't know what you're talking about, but if you want a rematch, it can be arranged!"

You catch the chairlift up together again, chatting and laughing the whole way. You'd forgotten how much you like Mitch. "You know," you tell him as you head over to the slope again, "I really miss you."

"I miss you, too," he admits, catching your eye before you both head down the steep slope again.

When you reach the bottom, Mitch slides over to you and grabs your arm. "Come on, they're about to close this place down," he says, pointing to where the sun is setting behind the mountain. "Let's go one more time."

You're starting to feel really tired and cold. And you'd like to just hang out with Mitch inside and catch up—something that's pretty hard to do when you're snowboarding. "I don't know…," you say. "My feet are freezing."

"Don't get all girlie on me now!" Mitch taunts you. "Night snowboarding—it's the best! Just a little bit longer.…"

You agree to board down one more time. Go to 151.
You'd rather try to get Mitch to come inside. Go to 155.

"Oh, I don't know if I'm good enough to race you," you tell Mitch, acting coy. Guys don't like girls who are too competitive, right?

"You're pretty good—c'mon!" he urges you. "Loser buys the winner a hot chocolate later at the café."

As much as you want to snuggle with him at the café and sip hot chocolate together, you just can't race against him. "No, you're way better than me," you say shyly, hoping to stroke his ego.

"Okay," Mitch says, moving into position to go down the slope again. A cute freckle-faced girl in a white baseball cap moves into place beside him. She's got on a great snowboarding outfit.

"Race you down?" she turns to Mitch and challenges. She gives him a flirty smile.

"You're on!" he says, and pushes off down the mountain without even looking back. As you watch them race down the slope, you can't help wondering if he's going to end up drinking hot chocolate with her in the café—*argh*! That girl is racing off with your crush, and you have only yourself to blame!

END

If you want to take Mitch up on his challenge, go back to 124.

"Okay, I'd like to try," you tell Travis. "If you don't mind showing me how."

"No problem," Travis says. He picks out a snowboard for you, and you all head over to the snowboarding area. "It's probably better to learn over here," Travis explains, "than head straight to the slopes."

"I'm going to hit the half-pipe," Mitch says, walking off without even saying goodbye. You're thankful that Travis is so sweet.

You look around at everyone else snowboarding—it looks simple, so you're sure you'll get the hang of it. But once Travis helps you get your boots hooked into the board, you realize that you have no idea how to even move!

Travis puts his hands around your waist. "You just have to lean your body forward, bend your knees, and move the board." He shows you how. He's leaning over you, talking so close to your ear that you can hardly pay attention. When you do move forward, you suddenly jerk straight up. "Bend your knees!" Travis yells, but when you do, you topple backward and land on your tailbone so hard that you see stars.

"Ohhhhh, ouch!" you say, feeling tears come to your eyes. And Mitch chooses just that minute to swing by.

"Dude, come hit the half-pipe. She can practice on her own," he tells Travis, who's busy helping you up.

"Why don't you practice what I showed you here on this small slope and I'll come back to check on you, okay?" Travis says.

"Sure," you tell him sadly. You understand that the guys came to have fun, not teach you how to snowboard, but you're still bummed. What happened to spending time with Mitch? Travis is the only one even paying any attention to you!

After almost an hour of practicing, you're exhausted—you're covered in snow, freezing, your butt is permanently numb, and your wrist hurts from falling down so many times.

"Hey, how's it going?" Travis slides by and asks you. "Hurt your wrist?"

"A little," you admit. "I'm not sure snowboarding is for me. It looks so easy for you and Mitch; I just don't know if I can get it," you say, snapping your boots out of the board.

"Don't give up—let's try again tomorrow. You just need to soak in the hot tub for a while, then you'll feel better—I promise," Travis says.

You pick up your board and turn to head back to the lodge. "Well, thanks for trying to teach me," you say glumly.

"Look, let me do two more runs on the half-pipe, and I'll meet you at the hot tub. After a good long soak, you'll be ready to try snowboarding again." He winks at you, and you feel a shiver go down your spine. Are you just cold, or does this guy like you?

Just then, Mitch slides by. "You quitting already?" he says to you.

"I'm spent," you admit, but you don't mention that you might be heading to the hot tub. And neither does Travis.

"Come on, man," Mitch says, pulling Travis by the sleeve. "Hey, we'll see you later on, maybe tonight or something," Mitch calls back to you.

Travis turns to go. "Really, two more runs and I'll see you there, okay?" he asks. You are feeling so sore and bruised, maybe a soak would do you good.

And you do want to hang out with Travis; you just feel funny doing something behind Mitch's back. Suddenly it hits you that getting into the hot tub with Travis means one thing: bathing suit! *Eeek*! Do you dare?

If you want to meet Travis at the hot tub, go to 153.

If you want to skip the hot tub, go to 157.

"Jenny's not always right about everything," Heather whispers to you.

"Then let's go meet the guys and we can decide for ourselves," you say. You both hurry to get changed, then race outside to look for Jim and his friend at the chairlift.

"Hey!" Jim yells over to you. They're already at the front of the line!

"Come on," his friend says, waving you over.

"Great," Heather says, catching her breath as you join the boys. "No waiting—I like it!" She grins at the redheaded guy.

"By the way, I'm Henry," he says, taking off his glove to shake her hand.

"What a proper gentleman." Heather laughs when he takes her hand and kisses it European-style.

You're glad that you decided to meet up with these guys—they don't seem so horrible!

"You're next," the guy running the chairlift turns and says to you...and Jim! *Oops*. Looks like you will be going on the chairlift with him, alone. Are you ready to be stuck, high up in the air, with this guy you just met—a guy who doesn't have a great rep? You could just step back and ride up with Heather, putting Henry on the lift with Jim. What should you do?

You decide to ride the chairlift with Jim. Go to 160.
You'd rather ask Henry to ride with Jim instead. Go to 134.

You just can't let your friendship stand in the way of fate! Obviously, Dan adores you—and he has forever. Maybe he's the one for you? You race down the stairs to the lobby to meet him, your face flushed with excitement. Yes, Heather will be mad at you for a little while, but once she sees how great you two are together, she'll have to realize it was meant to be.

As you look around the lobby for him, you're picturing how the rest of the trip will be—so romantic! You'll finally have a boyfriend, and you can't wait to show him off.

But then you see him, sitting on the couch. And he's not alone. There are two really pretty girls sitting with him.

"Hi," you walk over and say. "I'm ready to go skiing with you." You stand there, looking at him, and waiting for his explanation—there must be one, right?

"Oh, great!" he says, smiling. "You don't mind if Sharla and Colleen join us, do you?"

"I thought we were going to go skiing, um, just the two of us," you say, looking from one girl to the other. They both just give you a blank stare.

"What, and leave one of my girls here? No way!" Dan laughs. He stands up and puts his arms around Sharla and Colleen. "Come on, ladies," he says, then turns to you. "You coming?"

"No, thanks," you say. You race from the lobby as you feel tears stinging your eyes. So much for true love—you can't believe you compromised your friendship with Heather over this loser!

END

Want to rethink skiing with Dan? Go back to 135.

You go over to Heather and offer her a tissue. "Carrie, you're right. Dan is a total dog. I don't know what I was thinking." You sit on the floor by Heather, and look up at her. She's sniffling and her face is all red and blotchy. "Heather, I'm sorry. Really."

"That's okay," Heather says. "I'm not mad at you, I'm mad at Dan. And myself. How could I fall for such a jerk?"

"Don't blame yourself," Carrie says, pushing Heather's hair back from her face as she blows her nose. Just then, there's a knock on the door. "Oh no, I bet that's him!" Carrie says, moving to answer it. "I'm going to tell him to…" But when she jerks the door open, it's actually Mrs. Bulow standing there!

"I heard some yelling, is everything okay?" she asks, her eyes darting to Heather. "Oh no, what's wrong?"

"Nothing." Heather sniffles. "Just boy trouble,"

she laughs weakly.

"And we can't fix the stupid bed!" Carrie adds, and you have to laugh.

150

Go to 132.

You're on the chairlift when the lights start to snap on all over the mountain. "Yes! Night skiing!" Mitch says.

And you have to admit, it is amazing zooming down the slope on your snowboard in the dusk, the sunset casting a warm, pink glow over everything. The mountain gets quiet as everyone goes in for dinner, and you can hear the sound of your own breathing and your board swishing against the snow as you make your way down.

When you reach the bottom, you turn to Mitch. "Okay, let's go turn in this stuff and eat—I'm starving!"

"One more time!" he says, putting his gloved hands together in a begging motion. "Please."

"That's what you said last time," you laugh. "We're going to be late, and I'm really freezing." You're annoyed that Mitch doesn't seem to want to spend time with you anywhere but the slopes.

"This is really the last one," he says, giving you a sweet grin.

You decide to:

Say yes to one more run. Go to 170.

Tell him no, and head inside. Go to 155.

You stand in the snow, holding your board and watching Mitch and Travis head over to the half-pipe again. Mitch is pretty good, but Travis is amazing—he's zooming around, bouncing up off the sides of the ramp and catching air every time. *This guy wants to hang out with you*—the thought goes through your head, and you can't help but smile. He is smoking hot, and nice, too.

You return your rental board and head up to your room to change. But when you get out your bathing suit, you're filled with doubt again. It looks so tiny next to the big bulky jacket you've been wearing all day. You're going to be meeting Travis…in a bikini?

You tie on your top and look in the mirror. You're so pale! Well, it is winter, after all. You wrap a towel around yourself and sit on the bed. Are you ready to do this? That's when you remember that Heather brought some self-tanning lotion on the trip. You go into the bathroom and pick it up off the counter, then glance in the mirror again. A little tan sure wouldn't hurt. But do you have time to do this now? How long before Travis heads over to the hot tub to meet you?

You decide to try the self-tanner. Go to 163.
You'd rather skip it and head to the hot tub. Go to 164.

"Sorry, I've got to go in and warm up," you tell Mitch, hoping that he'll change his mind and come with you. "I guess I'll see you in there."

"Hey, are you mad at me?" Mitch says, sensing your mood.

"No, I'm just tired," you tell him. You're too embarrassed to tell him that you really want to eat dinner with him and sit with him by the fire. That's so girlie—something you know he can't stand!

"Okay," he says, and pushes off for the chairlift, looking over his shoulder at you as he goes. What happened? You guys had such a great day together, but now he's acting like he just wants to go his separate way. He'll probably eat dinner with his new friends from Marshall and act like he hardly knows you.

After you turn in your rental gear, you can't help yourself. You head over to the windows at the front of the lodge to watch the slope for Mitch's blue jacket. Maybe the problem is that he still just sees you as a friend. How can you get him to notice you as a girl, too? You let out a sad sigh as you scan the mountain for him. But it's so dark....

"Hey," someone says behind you. It's Mitch!

"What are you...I thought..." You point out at the mountain.

He shrugs. "It's just not as much fun without you," he admits, looking down shyly. "Besides, I didn't want to miss having dinner with you."

You grin at him. "Ready?" he says, taking your hand and leading you over to the dining hall. Maybe he has noticed that you're a girl after all!

END

You get back up to your room and take out your bikini and lay it on the bed. How could you ever wear *that* around Travis? Your face starts turning red just thinking about it—you hope Travis will understand when you don't show up. You decide to take a bath instead, maybe that will help with all your aches and bruises. And you're so exhausted from learning how to snowboard that you practically fall asleep in the tub! When you get out, you change into your favorite flannel pajamas and curl up on the bed. The guys made snowboarding look so easy—why are you in so much pain?

There's a knock on the door, and you think it must be your friends, back from the slopes. Wait until you show them your bruises!

But when you open the door, it's not your friends—it's Travis! "Oh...," you say.

"You didn't come down to the hot tub, so I thought I'd come see how you were," he says. He looks so different without his snowboarding stuff on—tall and thin, in jeans and a T-shirt.

"I'm okay," you finally say, "just sore." Then you realize that you're wearing your pajamas and you start to blush.

"I have just the thing for that," Travis says, holding out a paper cup. You take it in your hands and it's warm. Hot chocolate!

"This is so good, thanks," you say, taking a sip.

"If you're feeling up to it, you can come down and sit by the fire with me—some other girls are also wearing pj's, so you don't even have to change."

You look down at your fuzzy slippers and grin. You missed one chance to hang out with him because you didn't want him to see you in a bikini, and now you're wearing your pajamas! You can't help but laugh.

"What's so funny?" Travis says, looking at you with a smile.

"First you see me in a snowsuit, now pajamas," you tell him. "I'm feeling fashion-challenged around you, I guess!"

"You looked cute today," Travis says. "Even when you were falling on your butt! And you look even more adorable now." He leans in and gives you a tiny kiss on the forehead. Looks like you've landed yourself a snowboarding sweetie!

END

You take a look over at Jim—he seems nice enough. "Okay, you two," the guy running the chairlift yells, and you step up with Jim to get on. The guy closes the bar across both of you, then you're on your way.

As the chairlift pulls you up, you glance back down to Heather, who's so busy talking to Henry she doesn't even wave.

"So," Jim says, stretching his arm out around your shoulders. "How do you like the ski trip so far?"

"I'm having a good time," you tell him. "Haven't skied much, but I guess that's only part of the fun, right?"

"Exactly," Jim says, and leans in on you.

"Uh, what are you doing?" you ask him.

"Just having fun," Jim says in a slimy way as he moves his face closer to yours. You can smell whatever he ate for lunch on his breath.

"Not interested," you say, turning your face away.

"What, you've got a boyfriend or something?" Jim asks. "I won't tell if you don't." He gives you a smile that turns your stomach.

"I don't have a boyfriend," you tell him. "I just don't like you that way."

"Man! I knew I should have ridden the chairlift with your cute friend, what's her name again, Heather?"

You just shake your head at him. You can't believe you took a chance on this guy! Heather's friend was right—he's not the kind of guy you want to go skiing, or anywhere else, with!

END

Wish you'd never gotten on the chairlift with this creep?

Go back to 145.

"**O**h, I heard that Mrs. Bulow is outside, so I'm just getting my coat so that I can find her," you lie.

"Okay," Heather says.

"'Bye," you say as you go out the door. You feel terrible about lying to your friend, but then you remember that Dan liked *you* first! And he said he was just using Heather to get close to you.

You race down to the lobby to meet him.

Go to 147.

ou pick up the bottle of self-tanner and shake it hard, then spray it all over yourself as the directions say. Then you spray some on your face and rub it all around. It smells terrible, like burnt toast.

"There! Now I'm a real ski bunny," you tell your reflection as you wash your hands. And wait.

And wait some more.

It doesn't seem to be working, so you spray on a little more, then a lot more. You look in the mirror. You're still pale!

You read the back of the bottle again, carefully, and see where it says "...can take up to two hours to see results." *Grrrrrr!* Now what? Should you just head down to the hot tub looking ghostly white and smelling of self-tanner, or wait longer to see if this stuff works? You wonder how long Travis is going to wait for you....

You decide to just head to the hot tub. Go to 166.
You'd rather wait longer. Go to 168.

$\mathcal{Y}$ou put down the self-tanner and wrap yourself in a big, fluffy towel. That stuff never seems to work on you, anyway. When you get down to the hot tub, there are two other girls sitting in it, but Travis isn't there yet—perfect! You quickly drop your towel and climb in, letting the bubbles hide you.

Just as you get settled in, Travis shows up. "You look comfortable in there," he says to you as he slides into the hot water. "Whoa, this is really hot!"

"I think it feels perfect," you tell him, grinning. "Thanks for suggesting this—it's exactly what my bruises and bumps needed!"

"You did a great job for a beginner," he tells you.

"Really? Then why am I in so much pain?" you laugh. "Check this out…." You hold your knee up out of the water so that Travis can see the big purple bruise there.

"Man, that looks bad!" he says, touching your knee gently. "You're delicate, huh?" He rubs his finger over the bruise. "Probably because your skin is super soft."

You put your leg back down and notice that Travis is either blushing or just turning red from the water temperature. "Snowboarding is really hard at first, but you'll get it," he says. "If you want to, we can try again tomorrow, just the two of us...."

"No Mitch?" you say. Remembering how jerky Mitch had been to you today, you wouldn't mind.

"No Mitch." Travis grins. "I'll handle that. You just work on getting yourself back in shape for tomorrow. I'm checking that knee myself before I let you back on the slopes."

You look down at the bubbles in the tub and smile. Looks like someone has a sweet new snowboarding crush!

END

You wrap up in a towel and hope that by the time you get down to the hot tub, the self-tanner will have kicked in and you won't be so super pale.

When you get down there, Travis is already in the hot tub, so you quickly drop your towel and slide in. "Wow, this really is hot!" you turn to him and say.

"You'll get used to it," he says, smiling.

You lean back and close your eyes for a second, letting the warm water flow around you.

"Wait, what's that?" Travis says, and you sit up to see a greasy orange pool forming around you in the hot tub. Even the bubbles are turning orange! Travis pops one of them with his finger. "It smells like sunscreen or something," he says.

"Oh no," you exclaim, and put your head in your hands. "I'm so embarrassed!"

"Why?" Travis laughs. "What is it?"

"It's some self-tanner I used right before I came down," you explain. "I was just so pale, and you'd already seen me fall on my butt all day. I just wanted to look…I don't know, better."

"You were so cute today, even when you were falling down," Travis says, looking right at you. "You don't have to be tan for me to notice you—I noticed you the second I met you."

"Really?" is all you can manage to say.

Travis nods. "In fact, I was going to ask you if you wanted to snowboard some more tomorrow—just the two of us."

"I'd love to," you hear yourself say, before you can even think about it.

"Great!" Travis grins. "But no more self-tanner—we don't want to turn the snow orange, okay?"

You smile back at him. "I promise," you say. Looks like falling on your butt all day is a great way to get a date with a sweet guy!

167

END

You pace around the room for a while, then sit on the bed and open a magazine. But every couple of minutes, you go in the bathroom to look in the mirror and see if you're getting any tanner.

After about half an hour, you can almost see a difference. "Fifteen more minutes," you tell yourself, looking at the clock. You're just hoping that Travis won't be too bummed that you're so late. When you feel like you can't wait any longer, you wrap a big towel around yourself and head down to the hot tub.

When you get there, you see a couple of other kids you know from your school soaking in the tub already. "Hi," you say, sitting on a bench. It's so cold out here, but you want to wait for Travis to come before you climb into the tub. After a few minutes out on the deck, your teeth are chattering.

"Why don't you come in?" a girl in the tub asks you.

"I'm waiting for a friend," you tell her, shivering.

"Oh, was it that Travis guy? He wanted us to tell

you that he had to go," she says, climbing out of the tub and wrapping up fast in a towel.

"What?" you ask. "He was here already?"

"Yeah, for half an hour or so, but then some girl came by and he left with her," the guy says.

"Oh," is all you can manage to say. You look down and notice that your legs are finally looking tan. But Travis has already left—with another girl! What a waste!

END

169

If you're ready to skip the waiting game, go back to 163.

"*Well...,*" you say, pausing for a second. "Okay, but just one more! Then we go inside."

"Yes!" he says, leading the way over to the chairlift.

The guy running the chairlift helps you both in, and you notice that Mitch leans in and says something to him. "No problem," the guy says with a smile and looks over at you for a second.

"Thanks, man," Mitch says to him as the chairlift pulls away. *What was that about?* you wonder. You think about it for only a second, because then you notice the scene around you. At night, the view from the top of the mountain is amazing, looking down on the lodge and the lights along the slopes.

"Wow," Mitch says, as if he's reading your thoughts. "It's so nice here, I wish we could come here every weekend."

"I know," you agree. "I was just thinking the same thing."

He smiles over at you. "Then I could see you every weekend," he says, and you don't know what to say. The chairlift stops, and you notice that you're the only two people on the mountain—at least at this slope. You head over to the trail and get ready to start down, but just then the lights snap out and you're in total darkness!

"Oh no!" you squeal. "I can't believe this! We're stuck up here!"

Mitch goes to put his arm around your waist. "Don't worry, I'll protect you from the abominable snow creature," he laughs.

"You *knew* the lights were about to go out, didn't you?" you ask him, but you already know the answer. So that's why he wanted to come up here for one more run!

"Maybe," he says, looking sly. You can barely see his face in the dim light from the lodge down below.

"Oh Mitch," you say, shaking your head.

If you're angry with him for tricking you, go to 172.

If you think it's sweet that he wanted to be in the dark with you, go to 174.

"I can't believe you would do something like this! You asked the guy at the chairlift to turn the lights out on us!" you say to Mitch.

"I thought it would be funny. I'd get to see you alone for a second or two, with no one else around," Mitch says defensively.

"Yeah, in the pitch blackness! It's dangerous—how are we supposed to get down now?" you huff.

"We can see the lodge down there"—he points—"so that's enough light to get us down the mountain. Come on, it will be fun."

"No, thanks!" you yell at him. You snap off your snowboard and storm off, trudging through the snow back toward the chairlift, but when you get there, you realize it's not running! Everything on the mountain is turned off, and you're stuck up here. You turn back to the slope, but it's so dark, you can't find Mitch. Where is he?

You get back to the top of the slope and realize that he went down without you. Now you're all alone on the top of the mountain on a freezing cold night in the pitch black. Unbelievable! This is the last time you ever let a boy talk you into something just because he's cute!

END

Want to rethink that last trip up the mountain?
    Go back to 151.

"I can't believe you would do something like this!" You grin at him. "You are the sweetest guy I've ever met!"

"Oh come on," Mitch says playfully. "You mean you haven't had guys chasing you all over school since I moved?"

"No." You shake your head.

"I was thinking that you would definitely have a serious boyfriend by now," Mitch says, looking down.

"Well, you know, nothing too serious," you joke.

You can hardly see Mitch's face in the dark, but you can tell that he's smiling. "Let's head down and warm up by the fire," he says, reaching out to take your hand.

"It's pretty dark," you tell him. "I don't know if we can...."

But Mitch is already pulling you down the mountain. You somehow manage to hold hands and slowly make your way together. It takes forever, but when you reach the bottom, you're absolutely freezing. You snap off your board and bend over to pick it up. "It's so cold at night here," you say, watching your breath rise up into the night air.

"I know," Mitch says. He wraps his arms around you from behind in a big bear hug, squeezing you tight. "You're lucky I'm here to keep you warm."

You tip your head back and look up at the stars, sparkling in the crisp winter sky, and sigh. Looks like last year's crush is now your long-distance boyfriend—and you couldn't be happier!

END

You look out the window for a second, and then take a deep breath. "I want to ask you about something, but I'm kind of embarrassed," you finally admit.

"You can ask me anything," Alex says, his face serious. "Shoot."

"Well, it's about Sierra. She said something about you—"

"We used to go out," he interrupts you. "Did you know that?"

You shake your head. "Yeah, two years," he says, taking a sip of his hot chocolate. "Then we started high school this year and I don't know, something just changed. She started hanging out with different people, and so did I. We just weren't that into each other anymore, I guess." He shrugs.

"Wow, two years!" You don't know what else to say.

"She hates it when I flirt with other girls," Alex admits. "So I usually don't do it in front of her, but then I saw you today..." He blushes a little and looks out the window. "I knew if I didn't talk to you right away, I might not get another chance, so I just did it."

You watch his face while he's talking. You can't believe a guy you just met would be so honest and straight with you—and you love it!

"I'm glad you did," you say quietly.

He looks away from the window and right at you. "Yeah, me, too," he says, and takes your hand across the table. Now the quiet between you isn't awkward anymore—it's great, because you get to stare into his dark, dreamy eyes for as long as you want.

END

You take a deep breath and try to think of something to say. "So…," you start awkwardly. "You, um, seen any good movies lately?"

Alex laughs, "Actually, I've been really busy with school, and I'm on the football team, so…"

"Wow, you play football, huh? I never would have known by the way you throw a snowball," you tease.

"Ouch!" he says, laughing. "If you must know, I was going easy on you today—in fact, I want a rematch," he says, leaning over the table to tickle your side. "Tough girl!"

"Hey!" You scoot away from his hand, laughing, just as you notice someone standing by your table. "Oh, Sierra, hi," you say quickly.

"Oh man," you hear Alex say under his breath.

"What is wrong with you?" Sierra glares at him. "You promised me that you wouldn't do this on the school trip!"

"Do what?" you ask, confused.

"He hits on my friends because he knows it

drives me crazy!" Sierra says to you. "He saw a chance with you, because you're new, you didn't know about him. That's why I told you not to fall for it!"

"You really need to get over yourself," Alex says to Sierra.

"No, you're the one who cheated on me, and now you have to hit on every single one of my friends," she yells at him, her voice rising. "Why are you doing this to me?"

You push your chair back from the table and start to walk away, but Alex is so busy fighting with Sierra, he doesn't even notice. So much for meeting a "nice" guy on this trip!

END

If you'd rather ask Alex about Sierra yourself, go back to 100.

"**A**ctually, I think I would like to meet your friend—the one who needs a roommate," you tell Zac quickly, and he gives you a big smile. You know he's younger than you, but he's still really cute—and so sweet!

"Hey, Molly," he calls to the blond girl across the room. She looks up, then comes over to where you two are standing at the desk. "Do you still need a roommate?" he asks her.

"Yeah, I do." Molly smiles and looks over at you.

"Well, is there a reward involved?" Zac jokes. "Because I've found you one."

"Of course!" Molly says, and she looks genuinely happy. "The reward is a big, fat thank-you from me."

"Aw, shucks." Zac grins. "I'll see you guys later," he says, and walks off toward the stairs.

"Hi, I'm Molly," she says, turning to you, and you tell her your name.

"Zac seems like a great guy," you add, once you know Zac is out of earshot.

"He *is* a great guy—and so smart, it's scary!" she laughs. "So, we'll have a room with three beds. I asked my friend Sierra from Marshall High to join us, too, if that's okay," Molly explains.

"Marshall High?" you ask. That's where Mitch goes to school—maybe you can find out if he's on the trip! "Sounds perfect! Let's go check in!" you say.

Go to 29.

"It's so sweet of you to offer, but I think I'd rather just stay with my friend Heather," you tell Zac, and you see his face fall. Just then you see Heather from across the lobby, and she starts walking over to you. "Actually, that's her now!" you tell Zac. "But maybe I'll see you later or something?" you say quickly.

He smiles. "Yeah, that would be cool. Maybe we'll see each other, or, um…." You can tell he's scrambling for what to say.

"Yeah, sure." You nod to him, just as Heather runs up. "I'll see you," you call out as Zac walks away. Should you have made some plans with him?

"Where were you? What happened? I heard the van broke down or something?" Heather asks, pulling your attention away from the Zac situation.

"More than that," you whisper, "but I'll have to tell you later."

"And James?" Heather asks quickly, raising one eyebrow.

You shake your head. "A loser. And kicked off the trip!"

"What?" Heather practically screams. "I'm dying to hear the whole story!"

Go to 187.

When the bus stops, you turn to Heather and say, "You know what, I think I'd rather stay with someone else on this trip."

"Why? What's wrong?" Heather says, scowling at you. "Is it because of what I said about that Zac guy? I was just kidding...."

"It's not that," you explain. "I just heard that the new girl at school doesn't have anyone to room with. And honestly, I don't think I can stay in the same room with Carrie, you know how she gets on my nerves."

"Well, I guess it's okay, then," Heather says, grabbing her bag and moving to get off the bus. "As long as you're not mad at me or anything?" She looks you in the eye.

You smile. "I'm not mad. Maybe it will be good for us to hang out with other people on this trip. You know, we do spend a lot of time together at school."

"Okay"—then she puts out her hand and smiles at you—"deal," she says. "But we'll still hang out, right?"

"Of course," you say, and you mean it. When everyone gets off the bus, you search for Zac at the check-in desk. When you finally see him, he waves over at you.

Go to 180.

"Dan, I just don't feel right about this," you tell him. "Honestly, Heather has a big crush on you, and she's my friend. If you still like me, that's your problem, but I'm not about to do something that might hurt my friendship with Heather." You turn and walk away from him fast, before he can say anything back to you.

What a total dog! *Ugh*. You're wondering if maybe you should tell Heather about what happened, when you see Mrs. Bulow coming around the corner. "Oh, I was just looking for you!" you tell her.

186

"What's wrong?" she asks you, looking concerned.

"Nothing bad," you say quickly. "It's just that the third bed in our room isn't working—the Murphy bed. Do you think you could help us with it?"

"Of course!" Mrs. Bulow says. "Just lead the way."

Go to 132.

"I'm so psyched that we're going to be roommates!" Heather cheers, leading you up the big wooden staircase in the lobby of the ski lodge. "Come on, let's check out our room," she says.

You turn just in time to see a familiar face coming down—Mitch!

"Hey, you!" he says. "I was wondering if you were going to be on this trip!"

You stop on the stairs and look at him for a second. He looks exactly the same, with his brown shaggy hair and that amazing one-dimple smile that always makes you feel breathless. "We're just going to check out our room," Heather says, grabbing your arm to pull you out of your mini-trance.

"Yeah, we're going to look at our room," you say, then realize you've just repeated exactly what Heather said. You feel like such a dork!

"Cool," Mitch says. "We're in room three-twelve. Come by and check it out."

"We're in three-eighteen!" Heather says excitedly. "Practically neighbors!"

You can't think of anything to say, and suddenly you feel weird just staring into Mitch's dark blue eyes. "Well, okay," he finally says.

"Excuse me!" a guy behind him says, trying to get down the stairs.

"Oh sorry, man," Mitch says, and takes a few steps down to get out of his way. "So, maybe I'll see you later, or…"

"Definitely," Heather answers for you, pulling you up the stairs. "'Bye, Mitch," she says.

When he's out of earshot, Heather turns to you, "Boy, you've still got it bad for that guy! You were like a zombie!"

"I know," you say, feeling embarrassed. "I couldn't even think of anything to say!"

"Um, just a simple 'Hi, Mitch' would have been good!" she laughs.

"Did I look like a total idiot?" you ask her.

"Don't worry about it," Heather says as you reach the top of the stairs. "You'll have time to make it up to him!"

188

Go to 33.

Zac pulls off his headphones and says, "What did you say?" thinking that you were talking to him.

"Nothing," you say, then whisper to him, "The guy sitting next to me was about to hit you up for homework advice."

Zac glances over, then smiles at you. "I hope you told him that I'm on vacation."

You laugh. "Yeah, something like that."

After a few more miles, the bus driver pulls over at a rest stop, where about half the kids climb off, and Heather comes back to see you. "Hey, how do you like it back here?" She smiles.

"How do you like sitting with Dan?" you ask her back with a wink.

She smiles, then looks over at Zac. "Hi," she says.

"Hey." He nods to her, then turns to you and says, "I'll be right back." He scoots around you to get off the bus.

Once he's gone, Heather whispers, "Sorry we stuck you back here with that new kid."

"He's actually really cool," you tell her honestly.

"I don't mind sitting with him."

"Cool?" Heather gives you a skeptical look. "He's two years younger than us."

"He's a *year* younger," you start to explain just as Dan comes up behind Heather.

"I guess we should trade back seats now," Dan says to you, then looks over at Heather with a very lovey-dovey look on his face. "It's only fair, right?"

"Well...," you start to say. It is fair—you're halfway through the trip, so you should get to sit with your friend. But honestly you don't mind sitting with Zac.

You want to move back and sit with Heather. Go to 36.
You decide to stay with Zac. Go to 38.

ᴄCYLIN BUSBY

first chose a life as a book and magazine editor, before
going back a page and becoming a full-time writer instead.
She lives with two boys of her own choosing—Damon, her
husband, and August, her son, in Los Angeles.

ready for a few new boys to choose from?

Check out:

Date Him or Dump Him?
The Campfire Crush

Is it a summer fling or the real thing?
Only you can decide.

And don't miss:

Date Him or Dump Him?
The Dance Dilemma

Will it be the date of your dreams or
a dance disaster? It's all up to you!

The life of an Inside Girl is anything but ordinary.

Find out what it's like in this fun new series by J. Minter, the creator of *The Insiders*.

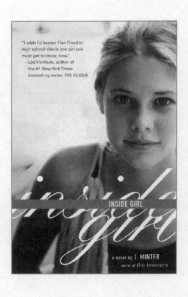

Flan Flood has always had her pick of the coolest parties and the cutest designer clothes. Her family is legendary in New York City, but she's sick of her friends hanging around just to get closer to her hot older brother, Patch. So when Flan starts at a new high school, she decides to reinvent herself as a totally normal girl. The only problem is, Flan's life isn't exactly normal. What will happen when her two worlds collide?

"I wish I'd known Flan Flood in high school—and not just because she has a hot older brother with hot older friends (although that totally helps). Don't let the name fool you—this is one girl you must get to know, now."

—Lisi Harrison, author of *The Clique*

Learn more about Flan and the Inside Girls at www.insidegirlbooks.com